Fear My Gangsta 3

A Novel by Tranay Adams

Fear My Gangsta 3

Copyright © 2019 Tranay Adams. All rights reserved.

Warning: The unauthorized reproduction or distribution of this work is illegal. Criminal copyright infringement, including infringement without monetary gain, is investigated by FBI and is punishable by up to five (5) years in federal prison and a fine of $250,000.

All names, characters, and incidents depicted in this book are products of the author's imagination or are used fictitiously. Any resemblance to actual events, locales, organizations, or persons, living or dead, is entirely coincidental, and beyond the intent of the author and publisher.

No part of this book may be reproduced or transmitted in any form or by any means, electronic or mechanical, including photocopying, recording, or by any information storage and retrieval system, without permission in writing from the publisher.

Fear My Gangsta 3/ Tranay Adams-1st ed. © 2019

Table of Contents

CHAPTER ONE

CHAPTER TWO

CHAPTER THREE

CHAPTER FOUR

CHAPTER FIVE

CHAPTER SIX

FEAR MY GANGSTA 3
Certified Cap Peeler

CHAPTER ONE

2012

Fear came out of the trees of the mountain top. He had a line with several fish he'd caught himself and a spear down at his side. He smiled from ear to ear when he saw Hahn who was sweeping the porch. He held up the fish he'd caught, and his master smiled at him, giving him a nod of approval. Just then, the smile disappeared from Hahn's face, and he looked beyond his pupil. Coming out of the trees he saw a big bear sniffing around. The beast's eyes landed on the fish that Fear had in his possession. Wondering what had caught his teacher's eyes, Fear glanced over his shoulder. When he saw the bear, his eyes bugged and the saliva in his mouth dried. He swallowed the lump of nervousness in his throat and gripped his spear tight, causing his knuckles to bulge.

Fear threw the line with the fish on it up towards a nearby tree. The hook of the line landed around one of the tree's branches.

"I'm going to get the rifle!" Hahn called out to Fear and ran back inside of the cabin.

The bear looked to the fish Fear had thrown up into the tree and then to him. He was pissed off that the fish were too high up for him to get. The animal's blackened claw extended out of its paws, and it stood up on its hind legs, roaring loudly. The beast's large wet tongue and sharp teeth were on full display. Seeing that the bear was in attack mode, Fear took his spear into both hands and mad dogged the bear. He then roared as loud as he could at it. Lowering his head, his nostrils flared, and he clenched his teeth, causing his jaws to pulsate.

The bear went charging at Fear and he went charging at it. As they were about to collide, Fear cocked his stick back and swung it against the animal's head. The wooden spear broke in half and splinters went flying everywhere. The bear came back down on its legs and rubbed the side of its head, whimpering. Seeing that he'd hurt the animal, Fear searched the ground for the other half of his broken spear. Finding it, he picked it up, approaching the beast. He did fancy martial arts moves with the sticks, as he and the bear circled one another.

"Raaaooorrrrrrr!" the bear roared loudly.

"Raaaooorrrrrrr!" Fear roared back at him.

Hahn, who Fear didn't know ran inside of the cabin, ran back outside with the assault rifle trying desperately to load in its clip. While he was busy with the sniper rifle, Fear and the bear charged one another again. The bear took several swipes at Fear, but he moved lightning fast dodging the ferocious animal's razor-sharp claws. Fear's training with the weights on his ankles and the stones in his backpack over time had him moving super swiftly. The bear couldn't touch him no matter how hard he tried.

Snikt!

The bear roared and took another swipe at Fear, tearing off the lower half of his shirt. Fear looked down at his ruined shirt and seemingly got angrier. Right after, he attacked the bear heatedly. He beat the beast's head and shoulders like a pair of drums, drawing wails of pain from it. He continued to strike the hostile bear upside its head and shoulders, until it eventually smacked both halves of the spear from his hands. Seeing that the animal was in close quarters of him and could seriously harm or kill him, Fear did back flips away from it. Once he stopped, he was a great distance away from the bear and had plenty of fighting room.

Fear ran over to some rocks he saw scattered not too far from one another on the ground. Kneeling, he started grabbing them and launching them in the bear's direction. The first one struck the bear in its head and caused it to holler out in pain. The second one struck the bridge of its nose while the others struck him in the forehead and temple. This further angered the bear and made him dizzy. It shook off his dizzy spell and went charging after Fear who took off running towards the cabin. In motion, Fear looked ahead to see Hahn locking a jacketed round inside of the sniper rifle. Seeing his pupil in danger, he tossed it up into the air at him.

Fear slid across the ground like he was trying to reach home base. Keeping his eyes on the rifle as he slid in the dirt, he lifted his hands to catch the high caliber weapon. Grasping it, he swung around to the animal as he was sliding in the dirt. The bear leaped into the air and Fear aimed upwards at it, looking through the scope of the sniper rifle. With one eyelid closed, he rested his finger on the trigger and waited until the beast's chest lined up with the crosshairs of his rifle. Once it did, he pulled the trigger and fire spat from his weapon.

Choot!

The bear fell to the ground hard. Lying on its stomach, it crawled after Fear hastily, trying to slash his legs with his powerful claws. Fear backed up in a hurry, repositioning his rifle so he could take another shot at it. Seeing the angry animal cock back its huge paw, Fear flipped over on his stomach and pointed his rifle at it. He squeezed the trigger, and the rifle shook, as it spat fire and spilled empty shell casings. The sharp missile shaped bullets took the beast's skull apart and blew his brains all over the fucking place. The bear dropped dead on the spot and Fear sighed with relief, relieving the trigger of the rifle.

Right then, Hahn came walking up. His shadow eclipsed Fear as he lay on the ground. He looked up at his master as he extended his hand downward. Fear got upon his bending knees and grasped Hahn's hand, letting him pull him to his feet.

"Are you, okay?" Hahn asked.

"Yeah, I'm straight." Fear nodded. He then brushed the dirt off his shirt and shorts. "What're we gonna do with him?" he asked of the bear he'd killed.

"Well, the cabin could use a good floor rug."

Fear chuckled and patted Hahn on his shoulder. "Come on."

Fear threw the strap of his rifle over his shoulder. He and Hahn then walked towards the slain bear.

Hahn went on to teach Fear any and everything he needed to know about the art of murder. After confronting death in the lynching, Fear's bravery had been solidified. He passed that little test easily. With that out of the way, Hahn went on to show Fear how to calm himself when critically wounded to slow his heart rate and blood flow so that he wouldn't bleed to death. Next, he demonstrated, with a knife, the points of the human body to attack to kill a man quick and proficiently. He also showed him the proper way to yield the knife and use it as a weapon. Once Hahn was sure that Fear had devoured his lessons, he moved him on to guns.

***

Glass bottles lined the log that lay on the ground. Fear watched attentively as Hahn placed the last empty glass bottle down on the log. He then pulled a handgun from off his waistline and screwed a silencer on the end of its barrel.

"This," Hahn held up the handgun with the silencer. "Is one of the most powerful weapons in the world."

Fear's forehead wrinkled and he scratched his temple, saying, "What's the other?"

"Your dick, Alvin Son, do you know why? Because your dick gives life, and your gun can take it." He answered his own question. "Today's lesson is about guns. Guns, guns, guns."

Hahn gave Fear the handgun he'd screwed the silencer on. He then stepped behind him. His face was masked with seriousness as he informed his student on how to properly hold a firearm. Fear was holding the gun sideways, so he had to show him the right way. "There you go. See now, the way you see them fools holding their guns in those hood movies is all wrong. You won't hit jack shit that way, but like this, this way not only the proper way to hold your weapon, but it also increases your chances of hitting your mark." Once Hahn was sure that his pupil had his aim locked, he went onto give further instructions. "Okay now. Spread your legs apart." He told Fear and he obliged. "Alright, I'ma step away now."

Hahn stepped from behind Fear and went to stand off to the side. He looked from his pupil to the glass bottle he was aiming at on the log. There was a moment of silence as she was making sure her sighting was lined up with her target. Then the explosions came.

Shatter!

Fear hit his first target and went on down the line to finish off the rest of them.

Shatter! Shatter! Shatter! Shatter!

The empty bottles exploded as bullets went through them, green glass and clear glass rained down to the ground. Fear lowered his smoking handgun and cracking a smile. He looked to Hahn who folded his arms across his chest and smiled, nodding his approval.

***

Fear practiced shooting the bottles a couple of more times. He then went on to practicing shooting moving targets. From there Hahn showed them how to kill someone up close.

"When executing a mark, it's always best to get 'em from afar, but if it's necessary to get close, then you wanna get just close enough." Hahn told him. "Not too close though. You see, you don't want his blood and/or hair follicles clinging to your clothing. Believe me when I say that forensics are a pain in the ass, you don't want your mistake to come back to haunt chu. Okay," he pointed his handgun with the silencer on its barrel at a dummy hanging from the same tree that he'd hung Fear from. The adult sized doll had a plastic head and a cotton, stuffed cloth body. The body had a diagram of human beings, mostly vital organs which were located on the left side. If any of these organs were to be severely damaged, death would be the result.

"Once you're close enough, give 'em one to the head," he pointed the gun at the dummy's head. "When he falls, stand back and give 'em two to the sternum to finish 'em off. You got that?"

Fear, who had a concentrated and determined look on his face nodded. "Good. Now, you try."

Hahn flipped the gun over in his hand so that the barrel would be in his hand and outstretched it towards Fear.

Later that day

Fear lay on his stomach beneath the shade of a tree. Hahn peered down below with an expensive pair of sleek, black, electronic binoculars. He worked the buttons and knobs on the side of binoculars and the front of it extended. Neon blue lights flashed on and off around its lenses. A green light stayed lit at the center of the binoculars and its antenna stood tall.

"Alright, there that cocksucka is. Just in time for his funeral."

Hahn sat the binoculars down and picked his silenced sniper rifle up from its opened case. He slid on the last attachments and chambered a missile shape jacketed bullet into the assault rifle. Having made sure, the deadly weapon was prepared, Hahn passed it to Fear, telling him how to hold and fire it. Fear took the sniper rifle and rested his eye against the scope. His face wrinkled with his concentration. "Alright now, line it up with either his chest or his head, whichever you please." He looked from the scope to the sighting of the rifle, trying to see if Fear was following his instructions. Through the scope there was a slim, white dude with tattoos over his face and arms. He was wearing a fishermen's hat and attire. He had a fishing pole in one hand and a line in the other. At that moment, he was heading back up to his cabin which was on the opposite mountain top. The line held several fish he'd caught. "You got it?"

"Yep, right on his chest."

"Excellent. Now watch his chest as it slowly rises and falls with each beat of his heart," Hahn coached him. "Watch closely, because I want you to become one with the beating of his heart.

Fall in sync with it, become one with it. You are it and it is you." He fell back for a few moments, allowing Fear to merge with the beat of the man's heart. Once he felt like they had become one, he continued with his coaching of him. "Now, very gently place your finger on the trigger, don't pull it just yet. Wait until that moment."

"What moment exactly?"

"*That* moment," Hahn replied. "I can't describe it, but you'll feel it when it comes. It'll let chu know when it's time to squeeze the trigger."

Choot!

The white dude dropped instantly.

Fear lowered the scope of the rifle from his eye, smiling. Hahn, who was very proud of him, patted him on his shoulder and commended him on a job well done.

"You executed him beautifully." Hahn told him. "Now let's get the shovels and stuff so we can bury him and see about collecting our earnings."

Fear switched hands with the sniper rifle and got to his feet, brushing the dirt from off his jeans. He then disassembled the rifle and placed it back inside of its casing. He shut the case, locked it and picked it up by its handle. Together, he and his master got the shovels and a bag of industrial strength lye so that they could bury their kill.

***

Once Fear and Hahn reached their kill, Hahn checked him to make sure he was the man that he'd been contracted to murder. The only way he had to identify him was through his tattoos. The photo that had been texted to his burnout cellular was of a younger man with hardly any ink. See, this may come as a surprise, but once Hahn found out he was dying, he got back into the murder for hire game. He planned on leaving his goddaughter and her daughter with as much money as he could so they wouldn't have any worries financially. He'd gotten the call to dispatch that poor son of a bitch at his feet the day before. It just so happened that he'd spotted him chopping logs for firewood a couple of days ago.

He couldn't believe the coincidence, but he was glad he'd be able to make some easy money.

The white dude that Fear had killed off went by the name, HittMan. He was a white supremacist hitta behind the wall that told on some very powerful people within his organization to guarantee his freedom. Once he was released, he had a bounty on his head, so he fled out to the mountains to escape street persecution. Unfortunately for him, he picked the very same mountains that one of the most dangerous men in the world had chosen to train his protégé.

"Yeah, this is him. Let's get to work." Hahn told Fear and took his shovel into both hands.

"Okay." Fear gripped his shovel with both hands and began digging.

Fear and Hahn dug a six feet deep hole. They threw Hitt-Man inside of the hole and covered his body completely in lye. They then shoveled the dirt upon him. Once they were finished, they rehydrated with canteens of water and made their way up to their kill's cabin. They cleaned the place so that there wasn't any sign of

his presence there and then they left.

***

Fear and Hahn made their way down from Hitt-Man's cabin, tired and dirty. Having finished up the job he was hired for, Hahn pulled out his burnout cellular and sent a text to his employer, letting him know that the contract had been fulfilled.

Afterwards, he stashed the cell phone in his pocket.

"I'll give you your cut outta the money you paid me for your training."

"Nah, you good. With the skills you teaching me, I'll be able to make that paper back and then some."

"Are you for certain?" he cracked a grin and threw his arm over his shoulders.

"Yeah, you leave that money to yo' family, we good."

"Thank you."

"Nah, thank you."

***

Hahn left the living room and came back with a haggard, thick, cherry brown book with a unique design engraved on its cover. The cover had a human skull with snakes coming out of its eye sockets and swords forming an X behind it. There were rusted gold hinges at both ends of it and a rusted latch with a pad lock attached. The book had information about killing that dated way back to the 1800s, during the medieval era, until present day.

Every killa that the book had been passed to placed new information inside of it, including its latest owner. Its information was priceless to an assassin. Hahn took a necklace from around his neck that held a golden skeleton key. He used the key to unlock the padlock and flipped the latch open. He then opened the book and turned it to Fear. On the first beige, tattered page was a long list of rules dating back centuries ago.

"These are the rules of L.O.E," Hahn started. "You will learn them for they are your gospel. And you shall adhere to them like they are the words of your Lord and Savior. Do you follow me?" Fear nodded, looking over the set of rules as his master went on. "Excellent," he nodded. "The penalties for breaking said rules are as follows." He slid a finger down the lines of penalties for breaking the codes aligning the page. Fear's eyes scrolled down the raggedy page. The punishments for violations ranged from whip lashings to beatings, to executions. "No one is above L.O.E, not even me." Hahn said. "You must follow the rules. If you violate them, you will face the underlying punishments. Got that?" "Fa sho'," Fear nodded.

"As part of your training, you will learn this book from cover to cover, just as I did." Hahn closed the book and set it on the tabletop. He then looped the necklace that held the skeleton key around Fear's neck and patted him on his shoulder. Right after, he left the living room and returned with a white towel and a Zippo lighter. Coming back inside of the kitchen, pulled open the cupboard above the stove. Reaching inside, he took down a bottle of Jack Daniel's. He then walked back over to Fear and pulled out a chair for him to sit down.

Having sat down, Hahn laid the towel over his leg. He then passed Fear the bottle of Jack Daniel's and opened up the lighter with a flick of his wrist. "Go ahead and drink it. It's best to get a nice buzz going before I proceed with this." he told Fear.

Fear looked from the Jack bottle to Hahn, forehead creasing. "What's all of this?"

"I'm gonna singe off the tips of your fingers and toes. Should you ever wind up in police custody, you'll be harder to identify."

"That's smart."

Fear twisted the cap off the Jack Daniel's bottle and took it to the head. His throat rolled up and down his neck as he guzzled the strong dark liquor. He brought the bottle down and wiped his lips with the back of his hand. Afterwards, he took the bottle to the head again until he felt himself becoming tipsy. Next, he placed his hand on the towel and lifted his fingers.

A flame sprung from the lighter once Hahn struck the round metal ball in a downward motion. He held Fear's fingers while he went about the task of burning off the tips of them. Fear grimaced and squared his jaws, feeling the bluish yellow flame licking up his fingertip. His foot tapped the floor slowly at first, but then it sped up the longer he felt the hot flame.

"Gaaa!" Fear's face balled up and he squared his jaws, vein bulging at his temple.

***

Hahn put A & D ointment on Fear's fingertips and toe tips. He then wrapped them in band-aids. Fear was as good as drunk now, which was fine by Hahn because he still wasn't done with him yet. After he snapped his Zippo lighter shut and snatched the blood splotched towel from his leg, he stored the items away and disappeared into the master bedroom. He returned shortly with a leather bag and sat it on the tabletop. Opening it, he began removing all of the tools and items he'd need to give someone a tattoo. Once he was done, he sat down in the chair he'd been in previously and placed Fear's hand on the tabletop. After preparing his tattoo-gun with ink, he cleaned Fear's hand with alcohol and started on the tattoo. When Hahn had finished, Fear had L.O. E inked on the side of his hand.

Fear looked at his tattoo smiling, drunkenly. He then laid his hand beside Hahn's tattooed hand. Both men wore the same ink. The only differences in the tattoos where Fear's was obviously fresher, while Hahn's was fading.

"What exactly does L.O.E stand for?" Fear questioned.

"Loyalty Over Everything, or League of Executioners," Hahn answered as he applied ointment to Fear's tattoo which his skin had swollen around.

"How many of y'all was it when you first started?"

"Including me? Five in total," He held up five fingers.

"Oh, yeah? What happened to them?" Fear asked, looking at his tattoo.

Hahn took a deep breath before answering Fear's question. "Gustavo had all of them killed. They joined forces to help me fight against his people, but they were all eventually murdered. That's when I went into hiding and found a new profession."

"Damn, I'm sorry for your loss." He looked upon him with sympathetic eyes.

"So, am I." Hahn said regretfully. He hated that he allowed his comrades to join him in his crusade against Gustavo. Had he kept them out of his personal affairs they may have all been alive today. "Go ahead and get started reading the book tonight. I'm gonna go ahead and hit the sack. Goodnight, Alvin Son." He patted him on his shoulder and journeyed back inside of his bedroom, coughing along the way. Suddenly, his legs buckled, and he fell against the wall, barely holding himself up.

"Master Hahn," Fear rose from his chair to go to help him. He took three steps before Hahn was lifting his hand, signaling for him to stop.

"I'll be just fine, son. Go ahead and start on your book." He pulled a handkerchief from out of garbs and held it to him mouth. He coughed into it as he headed towards his bedroom. Once he was inside his bedroom, he shut the door.

Sitting back down at the table, Fear picked up the book that Hahn had given him. He started reading it but hearing his master coughing as violently as he had stopped him. He wanted to go to his aid, but he knew he'd only turn him away. With that in mind, Fear went on to read the sacred book.

For the rest of Fear's stay up in the cabin, he studied the book. The book had information on the human anatomy, the human psyche, war tactics and strategies, amongst several other things.

***

Hahn faced Fear as they stood in the lake. His hand was on the top of Fear's head while the other was holding his arm. Today was the day that he was going to be baptized. His ceremony was taking place for him to be reborn…as a professional hitman.

Hahn gave a sermon that ended with, "Alvin Son, I hereby baptize you in unholy water," he dunked his student into the water, quickly pulling him back up.

Fear was soaked and beads of water were running down his face, dripping from off his chin.

Excited about having graduated to another level of the game, Fear hugged his master affectionately. Taken off guard by the sudden act of endearment, Hahn reluctantly hugged the youngsta back. He smiled proudly as he looked down at his pupil. Although he'd trained him to be the best at a very ugly trade, he was still impressed at how he'd taken to things. The art of murder seemed to be second nature to him. It was as if he was born to do the shit, and all he needed was the right guidance to recognize his gift.

That night

"I can tell y'all right now what these niggaz thinkin'." Reckless said as he stood before the last of Davino's foot soldiers. He took the time to take a pull from his burning blunt and blow out a cloud of smoke. He'd called a meeting at his girlfriend's house as soon as he heard about what happened to Davino. He told the soldiers about it and they were hot. They all had mad love for Davino. Not only did homeboy pay well, but he also often kicked in a few extra dollars to them on the love. "They thinkin' 'cause Davino and Buck are dead that our blocks are up for the takin', but I say they got us fucked up! What they don't know is they ain't takin' shit of ours! I got the plug in pocket so our corners are still gonna be rockin'! All we gotta do is lay these niggaz down, lay low for a while and get back to gettin' this money!" He walked over to the kitchen table in the crack house and mashed out what was left of the blunt. Next, he picked up an AK-47 and chambered a copper missile shaped jacketed bullet into its head. Turning to the collective, he continued to address them. "Now, I can go after these niggaz myself, on some one-man army type of shit, but I'm sure I'll be cut down before I take out the lot of 'em. So, I need y'all help. I need y'all to arm y'all selves and ride with me. Ride with me so we can get our corners back and ensure that niggaz eat." He looked around at all the faces gathered. All of them were twisted into hateful, vengeful expressions. "So, what's up y'all? Is y'all niggaz ready to ride with me and hold shit down, to guarantee that our families eat?"

"Yeah!" the collective said in unison. The men were either holding handguns or automatic weapons, which they held up in the air.

"That's what I'm talkin' 'bout y'all, now here's the plan…"

Reckless went on to tell his niggaz the strategy he planned on using in carrying out the executions of Big Sexy and his soldiers.

Food 4 Less parking lot

Big Sexy was leant against the side of his vehicle with his hands in the pockets of his jacket, waiting for Gunplay to arrive. It was 7:30 P.M, and he'd been there since 7 o'clock, the meeting time that he and Gunplay agreed upon. The giant found himself glancing at his Rolex occasionally, wondering why his young homie hadn't pulled up yet. Having gotten tired of waiting, Big Sexy turned around and opened the driver's door of his car. He was about to slide into the driver's seat when he heard someone driving up. Turning around, he saw a royal blue '96 Chevrolet Impala. The hood classic pulled into the parking space, two stalls over from Big Sexy's vehicle. Kurupt's *Girl's All Pause*, which had the automobile's trunk rattling, died as soon as the man behind the wheel murdered its engine.

Gunplay hopped out of his Chevy and slammed the door shut as he started in Big Sexy's direction. Reaching him, he dapped him up and gave him a gangsta hug.

"So, what's up, Big? What chu wanted me to do for you?" Gunplay asked as he rubbed his hands together. He wasn't cold or nothing. He rubbed his hands together like this out of habit.

"I gotta move I need you to make. You my number two so you the only one I trust to do this shit. And you can't tell anyone about this shit either, ya dig?"

"You dug, big homie."

"Good." Big Sexy ducked inside of his car and grabbed the package he had for Gunplay off the passenger seat. He then passed it to him. "Oh, and this is the address." He then reached inside of his back pocket and pulled out a folded piece of paper, passing it to Gunplay as well.

"Who am I 'pose to be giving this to? And what the hell is it, anyway?"

Big Sexy folded his arms across his chest and took a breath, saying, "That package is for Broli. I want chu to make sure he gets it."

"Look, Big, you know I'm not the type to be dipping all in a 'notha nigga'z business, but since I'm making this drop, I needa know what's this is about."

"It's about me getting out from under this nigga'z clutches."

Big Sexy chopped it up with Gunplay a while longer, before he found himself looking at his watch again.

"Yo,' I'ma get up witchu later. I needa get up outta here."

"Alright. And don't worry about nothing, cuz. I got chu faded."

Gunplay dapped him up and retreated to his car.

As Gunplay was starting up his whip and pulling out of his parking space, Big Sexy's cellular was ringing. He pulled it out of his pocket and held it to his ear as he pulled the door of his vehicle open.

"Who is this?" Big Sexy said into the cellular, slamming the door shut behind him.

"This Reckless."

"Reckless? Davino's people?"

"Yep."

For a minute there was silence. Big Sexy didn't know what to say. He was expecting Reckless to start talking big shit, threatening to kill him and shit, but he hadn't. At that moment, he wondered what kind of time the young nigga was on so he decided to play it cool.

"'Sup, nigga?"

"Look, man, I'm willing to let bygones be bygones." Reckless started. "I'd like to leave the past in the past and move forward. You know what I'm saying?"

"I feel you." Big Sexy switched hands with his cell phone. He then fired up his ride and backed out of the parking space, pulling off. "But what kind of guarantee do I have that you and yours ain't gone kick some more shit up, besides y'all laying face up in a coffin?"

"You don't." he admitted. "I don't expect you to take my word for it, either. But look at it like this. With the big homies being gone, I don't have anyone to keep hitting me off with work so me and my niggaz can eat. You on the other hand do. I figure if we make peace then maybe we can talk numbers, you feel me?" "Most def'," Big Sexy nodded.

"I'd like to give you a lil' peace offering. You know, so you know I ain't bullshitting here, and that I'm dead ass serious."

"When?"

"Shit, tonight if you up to it."

"Yeah, I'm up to it. Gemme an address." Big Sexy pulled the car over and parked. He popped open the glove-box and grabbed an ink pen and a napkin from out of it. Holding the cell phone to his ear with his shoulder, he held the napkin to the car's horn and jotted down the address he had requested. Once he'd done this, he looked the address over and nodded his head. "Alright, homie, I got chu. See you in an hour." He disconnected the call.

***

Reckless disconnected the call and looked up at the soldiers, rolling his AK-47 up in a blanket. He then slid his cell phone into his pocket and addressed the soldiers, "Alright, I got this sucka, ducka-ass nigga to agree to meet up with me. When he shows up, we gone slaughter his big ass…we gone do this shit for Davino." "Yeah, Davino." One of the soldiers spoke aloud.

"Okay then. Let's go see this bitch-ass nigga." Reckless motioned for the soldiers to follow him as he headed for the door.

The few of the soldiers that still had their guns out, tucked them shits on their waistlines and fell in step behind Reckless, walking towards the front door.

Italia pushed open the glass door of Planet Fitness as she crossed the threshold. She made her way through the parking lot, zipping up her jacket and adjusting her purse strap on her shoulder. Seeing her vehicle in her sights, she pulled out her car keys and unlocked the car. The locks popped and she made her way around to the driver's door. She pulled open the door and jumped in behind the wheel, sitting her purse on the front passenger seat. She had just stuck her key into the ignition when she locked eyes with a pair of menacing ones in the back seat.

"Fear?" Italia gasped her lover's name. Her eyes bugged and her mouth dropped open. Although it was her fiancé in the

backseat, she could feel that there was something off about him. She found her heart thudding and stomach turning.

Italia went to throw open the door and run, but he snatched her back inside of the car by her hair. Italia kicked and tried to pry his gloved hand from her hair, but her efforts were useless. Her assailant held a folded rag over her mouth. Instantly, she smelled an intoxicant on the rag which had begun to suffocate her. Her nostrils burned and her vision became blurry. She fought on desperately, but her movements began to slow. It was then that she found herself coming in and out of consciousness. Her eyes rolled to the back of her head, and finally, she slumped in her seat.

***

Verna, Fear's mother, came pushing her shopping cart out of the supermarket. She made her way across the parking lot, walking past an automobile that was pulling out of its space. Having made it to her car, she popped the trunk and started putting shopping bags inside of it. Unbeknownst to her, in the back of her, a man wearing a hood and a bandana over the lower half of his face was pretending to rifle through the trunk of his vehicle for something. But what he really was doing was dousing a rag with a substance from a small brown bottle. Once he was done with the bottle, he screwed the top on it and stuck it inside of the pocket of his hoodie. He then looked up and down the parking lot. Seeing that there weren't any witnesses in sight, he crept up behind Verna and suffocated her with the rag. Verna reacted the same way Italia had when she met the intoxicant. Before she knew it, she was going limp in her assailant's arms, and he was dragging her back towards the trunk of his vehicle. He duct taped her wrists and ankles. Next, he dropped the roll of duct tape inside of the trunk and slammed it shut. Afterwards, he straightened out his clothing, and looked up and down the parking lot to see if anyone was around to have seen him. Confirming that there wasn't anyone around, he walked around to the driver's door of his whip and pulled it open. Jumping in behind the wheel, he cranked up his ride and pulled out of the parking space.

CHAPTER TWO

Fear had finally completed his training and it was time to go home. He and Hahn packed up their stuff and made their way down the stone steps. They loaded their bags into the trunk of Hahn's Buick and climbed inside of the vehicle. As soon as Hahn pulled off, Fear powered on his cellular and hit his people up. The first person he called was Italia. The entire time her phone was ringing he was smiling from ear to ear. Hahn looked over at Fear and smiled. He knew that smile on a man's face too well. It was a smile only a special woman could give a man. It was a smile of love.

Italia's phone rang and rang until her voice mail picked up the call. As soon as the recording finished, Fear left her a message.

"Hey, lover, guess who's on their way home, I'll see you in a couple of hours. I love you." Fear said into the cellular and then disconnected the call.

As soon as Fear hung up, he got a text message from Big Sexy that erased the smile from off his face.

By the time u read this u will have finished your training.

Congrats! I'm gonna need you to put those new skills to use. I got a situation. Meet me here at 9 tonight...

Big Sexy went on to give him the address of the location. Fear memorized the address and turned his cell face down in his lap. He then massaged his chin as he stared out of the window, watching the scenery change before his eyes.

Hahn looked back and forth between him and the windshield, brows wrinkled. "What concerns you, Alvin Son?"

"My homeboy, Sex, has a situation back home," he informed him. "I gotta bring out the guns."

"So soon, huh?"

"Yeah, but that's my nigga, I'ma always bust my guns for 'em, you Griff me?"

"I got chu…loyalty over everything."

"That's right."

Having said that, Fear let his seat back and shut his eyelids. He knew he'd be back in the thick of the streets once he reached the city again, so he wanted to get as much rest as possible, so he'd be prepared for what lay ahead.

***

Hahn pulled his Buick up in front of Fear's house and put the car into park, allowing it to idle. He then nudged his pupil awake. Fear winced as he opened his eyelids. He yawned and stretched his arms. Afterwards, he put the seat up in its proper position. Turning around, he dapped up Hahn and thanked him for training him. He then hopped out of the car and made his way around to the rear of it. As soon as he heard Hahn pop the trunk open, he lifted it and recovered his duffle bag. He started towards his house, but hearing Hahn honk his horn at him, he turned around. The old man motioned for him to come back to his car, and he obliged him, coming to the driver's window.

"Take these," Hahn handed him a cell phone, a copper key and a folded note.

"What's all of this for?" Fear's forehead creased.

"The key is to my home out in Paramount. The address is written on that piece of paper." Hahn told him. "Down the basement there's a secret door. Search for the hollow sounding space on the wall, knock on it like this…" he knocked on his vehicle's dashboard in a special rhythmic pattern.

"Inside you'll find every weapon and disguise I used while I was in the game. They are all yours now."

"Thanks, Master Hahn." Fear said. He then held up the cellular phone he'd given him. "And this?"

"I got all my jobs through that cell. It never stops ringing." He informed him. "Keep in mind, son. The day you answer that phone and take a contract, there's no turning back. You'll be walking through a door that you can't walk back through. You understand?"

"Yes, Master Hahn."

"Good." Hahn replied and put his car into drive, indicating to Fear that he was about to drive off.

"Text me your goddaughter's home address. I'm gonna come by to check on you from time to time."

"Will do."

Fear walked away from the car, but it never pulled off. Suddenly, the driver's door of the Buick swung open, and Hahn stepped out. He turned in Fear's direction, seeing his back as he

walked away from him.

"Alvin Son," Hahn called out to him. When Fear turned

around, he found his master with his arms open. "I'd like a proper goodbye."

In that moment, Fear dropped his duffle bag at his feet and sped walked over to Hahn. He hugged him like a father would his son. When Hahn tried to break their embrace, Fear held fast to him, not wanting to let him go. Acknowledging this, Hahn grinned and continued hugging him.

"I'll see you soon." Fear told Hahn, teary eyed.

The old man nodded and jumped back behind the wheel of his Buick. He threw his vehicle into *drive* and pulled off.

With a heavy heart, Fear slung the strap of his duffle bag over his shoulder and trekked back towards his house. The tears that were in his eyes eventually slid down his cheeks. His weeping was due to Master Hahn pending death. He could tell by his physical appearance and his diminishing health that he didn't have much longer to live. He loved the old man like a second father. He taught him so much about life and other things. Just like his biological father had. When he was finally laid to rest, he knew that another part of him would die that he could never get back.

Fear unlocked the door of his house and crossed the threshold. Shutting the door behind him, he took a good look at his place. Everything was how he'd left it, and it was clean. It also smelled of Vanilla incents. He owed his thanks to Italia.

Not only could the girl cook. She cleaned, ran his bath water, ironed his clothes, supported his dreams and fulfilled his needs sexually.

Thinking of how he had a damn good woman by his side brought a smile to Fear's face. Before he knew it, he had crossed the living room and picked up the portrait of him and Italia sitting on the mantle above the fireplace. Seeing her face caused him to smile further. He couldn't help thinking of how blessed he was to have her in his life. She was his one and only. His ride or die. His everything.

"I love you, lil' mama," Fear kissed Italia's face on the portrait. He then sat it back down where he'd got it and headed to his bedroom. Dropping his duffle bag at the foot of his bed, he undressed and took a shower. Once he hopped out, he snatched the towel from off the rack and dried off. He threw on his underwear and opened his closet. He took a gun case down from the top shelf of the closet where he had it hidden behind some books and among other stuff. He sat the gun case down on his bed and popped its locks. When he opened it, there was an Uzi and three magazines and a box of ammo.

Having made sure his Uzi was still there, Fear headed back inside of the closet. He pushed the clothes that were hanging on the rack aside and revealed a sheathed katana. He picked up the katana and searched through the clothes. Finding his duster, he grabbed it by the hanger it was hanging on and brought it out of the closet. He threw the duster on the bed and stepped before his dresser's mirror. Holding up the katana, he drew it from its sheath and the light kissed off its blade. The sharp, shiny metal gleamed blindingly.

Fear tossed the sheath upon the dresser and positioned himself, holding up the katana. Right then, he practiced swinging the deadly blade like he had been trained to do.

"Yeah, this definitely not what niggaz want!" Fear said of his skills with the katana. He knew with all of his training that he'd be a force to be reckoned with.

***

Gustavo was shiny from sweat as he ran on the inclined treadmill, huffing and puffing. He had earphones in his ears and his cellular was attached to a Velcro strap-on around his arm. Occasionally, he'd snatch the white towel from off the handlebars of the treadmill and wipe his face and chest off. He'd then place it back on the handlebars and keep running. Hearing his cell phone ringing, he took it off the Velcro strap-on around his arm and looked at the display. Seeing who it was, he programmed the treadmill to be vertical and slowed it down. Walking briskly, he answered the incoming call.

"Mr. Cryler, I hope you have some good news for me," He spoke aloud, continuing his walk on the treadmill.

"I couldn't locate Hahn, it's like the guy fell off the face of the planet. However, I was successful in tracking down his goddaughter and her daughter." The P.I reported.

"Well, that's exceptional news." Gustavo smirked. He knew that by finding someone related to Hahn he'd eventually find him.

"I'm glad you're pleased, Mr. El Rey."

"Bring whatever information you have on her tonight."

"You got it. I'll be over just as soon as I drop my daughter off at her mother's house."

"Good. See you then."

Gustavo disconnected the call and placed his cell phone back on his arm. A smile stretched across his face as returned the treadmill back to its original settings and continued his exercising.

I'm coming for you, you black bastard. Full speed ahead!

***

Big Sexy pulled to the back of the warehouse where he'd been told by Reckless to meet him. He looked around but he didn't see anyone. His brows furrowed and he picked up his cellular, flipping it open. He redialed the number that Reckless had hit him up from earlier that night. Reckless picked up on the second ring. "'Sup wit it?" Reckless said into the cell phone.

"'Sup? Yo,' where you at? I'm here." Big Sexy told him.

"For real? I'm here. Nigga, where you at? I don't see you."

Big Sexy looked ahead through his windshield and then through his back window. His brows furrowed further, and he said, "I don't see you out here, man."

"It is pretty dark out here. Flash yo' headlight for me, homie."

Big Sexy did as he was instructed. As soon as the headlights flashed, Reckless appeared on the driver's side of his vehicle with his AK-47. Seeing something out of the corner of his eye, Big Sexy turned around to see his crafty ass. Reckless smiled wickedly behind his ski mask and pulled the trigger of his assault rifle. The automatic weapon vibrated in his gloved hands as it spat fire, empty shell casings dancing on the ground. When Reckless let up off the trigger of his AK, his eyes bulged, and his mouth dropped open. His firing on Big Sexy's automobile had only left scratches behind.

At that moment, Big Sexy came out of the sunroof of his vehicle gripping an AK-47 and laughing his ass off. He knocked on the windshield of his vehicle and said, "Bulletproof, mothafucka!" he then scowled at Reckless and started busting at his ass. His automatic weapon shook in his hands as it spat flames at his enemy. Reckless ducked and ran. He dove to the ground, tucking and rolling like a ball of hay. While in motion, he pulled out a grenade and sprung to his feet, swinging his AK around and spitting heat at Big Sexy. While this was going on, Big Sexy was reloading his AK-47. His was quite a distance away and Reckless's aim wasn't accurate, so he missed. Reckless's bullets deflected off Big Sexy's automobile.

"Bulletproof, huh? Well, how about grenade-proof, dicksucka!" Reckless snatched the ring out of his grenade and rolled it towards Big Sexy's car. Seeing the grenade rolling towards him, Big Sexy hurriedly climbed out of the sunroof of his vehicle. Kneeling on the rooftop of his vehicle, he leaped just as the grenade stopped underneath his car. Right as he leaped, the impact from the explosion lifted his car off its tires and landed it on its rooftop.

Big Sexy hit the ground hard and grimaced, still holding tight to his AK-47. Lying where he was on the ground, he looked up, trying his best to see through the smoke and flames. Through narrowed eyelids he saw Reckless making calculated steps towards him, his AK aimed at him. The son of a bitch was smiling as wickedly as he was before, feeling like he had the giant at his mercy, which he did. Big Sexy, still wincing, looked down at his leg. He could tell from the painful sensation in his ankle that he'd sprung it in the fall.

Reckless stopped where he was, standing over Big Sexy with his AK pointed down at him.

"This is for Davino!" Reckless's terrifying eyes bored down at his enemy as he clenched his teeth, flexing the muscles in his jaws.

Reckless was about to pull the trigger of his AK when he was suddenly blinded by the headlights of several automobiles. A group of vehicles swarmed into the location. Reckless knew that these weren't the cars of his homeboys so that meant they had to belong to Big Sexy's crew. Figuring this, he looked to where Big Sexy was and he had disappeared, leaving his AK-47 behind on the ground.

"Shit! I fucking had his ass!" Reckless cursed. He hated himself for not laying Big Sexy down when he had the chance.

Hearing someone coming from the side that the vehicles of Big Sexy's homies were approaching from, Reckless looked in that direction to see a handful of them niggaz hopping out of the cars, automatic weapons in hand. When they spotted him, they opened fire on his ass. He ducked and ran, letting his AK spit fire at them as he retreated. He found cover on the side of the warehouse and whistled. Right then, his niggaz appeared from out of the shadows.

They were all masked up and carrying firepower.

All hell broke loose as gunshots consumed the air and bullet shell casings deflected off the ground. Brain and skull fragments flew, and so did blood. Droplets splashed on the ground and left burgundy stains behind. Several bodies dropped as Big Sexy's and Reckless's men exchanged gunfire.

Although Reckless had lost a couple of his men, Big Sexy's niggaz were getting their asses kicked. In fact, there was only two of them niggaz left.

Reckless licked his chops as he watched his homeboys massacre the opposition. He looked to his left and saw Big Sexy duck down beside another car. He was pulling a handgun from the small of his back and checking the magazine of it to make sure it was fully loaded. Seeing that it was loaded, Reckless smacked it into the butt of his gun and cocked that bitch. He then slowly crept along the car Big Sexy was stashed beside. Looking from Big Sexy to his homeboys, Reckless saw that the giant had his sights set on them. His homeboys were so occupied with their firefight that they had neglected to watch their own backs.

"I see yo' ol' slick ass," Reckless swung out from the side of the warehouse, gripping his AK. He slowly crept upon Big Sexy. He lifted his assault rifle to spray his ass to death, but something happened that took him off guard. "Gaaah!" His eyes bulged and his mouth hung open. Blood pooled in his grill and dripped on to his gray hoodie. He looked down and saw a katana sticking halfway out of his chest. Before he knew it the ground was moving fast below him. It appeared as if he was flying but he was being driven.

Reckless threw his head back screaming bloody murder. He dropped his AK-47 as he was driven forward. The assault rifle went tumbling backwards on the ground hastily. Fear had come around the corner of the warehouse on his motorcycle and drew his katana. He sped towards Reckless as he was about to murder Big Sexy and thrust his katana threw his chest, driving him along on his motorcycle for a minute.

Snikttt

Fear snatched his katana from out of Reckless's chest and he fell to the ground, tumbling backwards. He then sheathed his sword and pulled out an Uzi. As he went to point his automatic weapon, the last of Big Sexy's men were being murdered. Just as the last man on Big Sexy's street team dropped dead, Fear pulled the trigger of his Uzi, waving it around. Some of the bullets shattered the windows of the vehicles that crowded the war zone, but the others met their intended targets, Reckless's men. The men hollered out in agony as bullets went through their bodies, causing them to dance on their feet. Once the last of them niggaz hit the ground, Fear stopped his motorcycle. He kicked the kickstand down with the heel of his boot and his bike leaned against it. Switching hands with his Uzi, he unsheathed his katana again. He made his way over to the men he'd shot up. The few that were still living, he finished them off, stabbing them through their hearts with his sword. Once he's stabbed the last breathing man, he did a 360, looking around to make sure not a soul among them was still alive. There wasn't, so he wiped his sword off on one of them and sheathed it at his back.

Fear looked over his shoulder and saw Big Sexy approaching him. The giant walked completely around him, looking at him in awe, touching the duds he currently had on. Fear was in a duster, Kevlar bulletproof vest, green cargo pants and boots. A bandana covered the lower half of his face to conceal his identity. Still, Big Sexy knew his best friend. It was through his mannerisms and the look in his eyes that he was able to identify the man that had just saved his ass single handedly.

"Damn, it's really you, huh?" Big Sexy said, like he couldn't believe it was him. While he was talking Fear was busy reloading his Uzi.

Fear pulled the bandana down from the lower half of his face, looking his homeboy in his eyes. "Yeah, it's me. I got cho text. Tonight, marks one year from the day I checked into those mountains. I left a changed man."

"I see." Big Sexy nodded and gave him a brotherly hug. "I missed yo' itty bitty ass, man. It's good to see you back home." He patted him on his shoulder.

"Uhhhhhhhh!" Reckless's moaning in agony drew Big Sexy's and Fear's attention. They looked over their shoulders and found him trying to pull himself up. His bloody hand grabbed the side view mirror of a nearby car, and he pulled himself upon his feet. He staggered forward and fell to the ground again.

"Excuse me, but I'm gonna have to cut this lil' reunion short. I have something that warrants my undivided attention," Fear brushed past Big Sexy and headed in Reckless's direction, Uzi down at his side. When he finally found himself upon Reckless, he was lying slumped against the car he'd fallen near. Blood dripped off his chin as he held the wound in his chest with both hands. He coughed up blood and looked up to the man whose shadow eclipsed him. Spotting the Uzi down at his side, he knew he'd come to finish him off, and he was willing to accept his fate.

Fear pointed the dangerous end of his Uzi at Reckless. He was about to pull the trigger when Big Sexy touched his wrist and insisted that he did the honors. Fear obliged his homeboy and stepped aside. At this time, Big Sexy was left standing over a slumped Reckless. Seeing that this was the end for him, Reckless shut his eyelids and said a prayer, crossing himself in the sign of the holy crucifix.

Blatatat!

A quick spray of the Uzi ceased all Reckless's movements and sent him wherever the fuck Davino went when he was murdered. Once Big Sexy had finished his enemy off, Fear took the murder weapon away from him and tossed it aside. He then motioned for him to follow him as he ran back towards his motorcycle. He mounted his bike, kicked the kickstand up and revved that mothafucka up. Afterwards, he motioned for Big Sexy to climb onto the back of the bike and passed him the helmet. Once the giant had put the helmet on, Fear sped away from the bloody crime scene, leaving smoke from his exhaust pipes in his wake.

***

The sound of Fear's speeding motorcycle filled the air as he flew up the street. He was going so fast the wind ruffled him and Big Sexy's clothing. Fear listened intently as Big Sexy filled him in on how he ended up staying in the crack game after his departure. The only detail he left out was the deal he made with Broli to save his ass. What the fuck did he look like telling Fear he sold him out so he could stay his black ass out of prison? There wasn't any doubt in his mind that he'd kill him as soon as he got off his motorcycle.

"What did he have on you?" Fear inquired, zipping past cars in traffic. His sights were set on the freeway, and it was getting closer and closer.

"Crooked mothafucka planted a brick on me." Big Sexy told him. "He told me as long as I moved weight for 'em, I'd stay a free man. I sure as fuck wasn't going to argue with that. I had to do what I had to do to keep my ass outta the fire."

"I feel you. Ain't no shame in that."

"I'm glad you understand the position a nigga was put in."

"Of course, I would have done the same thing." Fear confessed. "I mean, shit, it ain't like you ratted a nigga out. You Griff me?"

Big Sexy was silent for a moment before he answered. "Yeah, it's a big difference."

"Look, we gotta come up with a plan to get this nigga outta our hair. I can't move how I want as long as this nigga around."
"Don't worry about 'em. He's already being taken care of."

Vroooom!

The motorcycle ripped up the street.

***

Gunplay parked his car across the street and four houses down from his destination. He threw his hood over his head and popped open the glove-box, removing a package. After shutting the glovebox, he hopped out of the car and slammed the door shut behind him. He then looked up and down the street before crossing it. He walked briskly down the sidewalk, tucking the package in the back of his sweatpants. Pushing open the gate of a white two-story house, he entered the yard glancing at the car parked in the driveway. It was a BMW. This confirmed that the nigga he had come to see was indeed home. Acknowledging this, Gunplay walked upon the porch and knocked on the black iron screen door. While waiting for someone to open the door, Gunplay occasionally looked over his shoulders. Once he heard the locks of the door coming unlocked, he turned back around in time to see Broli standing before him. His muscular form filled out a wife beater and the denim jeans he was rocking were hanging slightly off his ass. Gunplay noticed his eyes were hooded and red webbed, and the stench of marijuana coming from him was overwhelming.

Broli brought a withering blunt to his mouth and sucked on the end of it. He then blew out a cloud of smoke into the young nigga'z face. Gunplay didn't bat an eyelash as the intoxicating smoke submerged him.

"Fuck is you doing here, lil' nigga? And more importantly, how the fuck you know where I lay my head at?" Broli asked in a threatening manner. Gunplay started to buck on him, but he thought better of it once he noticed the handgun in his hand.

"I got something for you. Big Sexy thought that it was imperative for you to see it." Gunplay pulled out the package and held it before Broli's eyes, wagging it.

Broli stuck the blunt into his mouth and snatched the package from Gunplay's hand, saying, "Fuck is this, a porno?"

"Nigga, you really think my black ass came all the way over here to deliver you a fucking porno? Come on now, cuz. Don't try to play me." Gunplay stuck his hands into the pockets of his hoodie.

"Bring yo' ass on in, man." He motioned for him to come inside his house with his handgun. Once he did, he shut and locked the door behind him. Afterwards, he led Gunplay into his living room where he popped the disc inside of a DVD player and turned on the flat-screen television set. Broli sat down on the couch while Gunplay stood, hands still in the pockets of his hoodie, watching the screen.

Broli blew out a cloud of smoke and mashed out what was left of his blunt in an ashtray on the coffee table. He watched the television screen as he dangled the remote control between his legs. What was playing out on the screen before him caused his brows to wrinkle, and he looked at Gunplay eerily. He then focused back on the television. He saw Big Sexy walking away from him as he pointed a gun at Davino and shot him to death.

"Say, bruh, what the fuck is this shit?" A pissed off Broli threw the remote control at the flat-screen and cracked its monitor. He was on his feet now and pointing his gun at Gunplay. His eyebrows arched and his nose scrunched up. His jaws were clenched and throbbing. Seeing himself in the footage murdering a mothafucka had totally blown his high.

"Easy, tough guy," Gunplay said. His hands were still in the pockets of his hoodie as he stared into Broli's face. The young nigga didn't even break a sweat. It didn't appear to bother him that his life was being threatened. "You bust a cap in my ass, and the big homie gone make sure that footage gets sent to every news station in Southern California."

"That slimy fat-back fried chicken eatin' cocksucka." Broli said under his breath, still pointing his gun at Gunplay.

"Now, look, in order for this footage to stay outta the public's eye," Gunplay began. "My man is gonna need you to lay off 'em. That means falling the fuck back and letting 'em run thangs how he's been running 'em...without yo' input of course."

"What about my cut?"

"Ain't no mo' cut, cuz. Big is severing ties with you." Gunplay told him. "And if you decide to do anything besides destroy that evidence you got on 'em, he's gonna use that footage to make you famous."

A defeated Broli lowered his handgun at his side and bowed his head, massaging the bridge of his nose. Big Sexy had a handful of his nuts and he was squeezing them. He knew if he didn't want them to rupture, he'd better leave him alone.

Gunplay walked over to the coffee table and picked up the blunt that Broli was smoking earlier. He sparked up the blunt and took a few drags from it, blowing smoke into the air.

"This is some primo shit chu got here." Gunplay looked at the burning blunt. He then looked back up at Broli, "You gotta shoot me yo' connect's number, pronto, cuz."

Broli's hateful eyes darted up to Gunplay, motioning towards the door with his gun, he said, "Get the fuck outta my house."

"Say no mo'." Gunplay walked down the hallway towards the front door, taking drags of the blunt all the way.

***

Hahn pulled up in front of his granddaughter's house and killed the engine of his vehicle. Hopping out of the car, he made his way around to the trunk and opened it with his key. He took a cautious look at his surroundings before lifting the trunk open and grabbing the duffle bag out of it. He hoisted the strap of his duffle bag over his shoulder and shut the trunk. He stepped upon the curb and made his way towards the house, keeping a watchful eye out as he adjusted the baseball cap on his head. He straightened out the sleeve of his jacket and fixed the collar of it as he proceeded towards the house. Making it upon the porch, he lifted his fist to knock on the front door but froze his hand at it. His brows crinkled up when he saw that the front door was already cracked open. Taking note of this, he pulled out his gun and gently pushed the front door open. All the lights were out inside of the house, but the lights from the posts lining the street illuminated the living room. This showed his granddaughter and her daughter lying on the floor of the living room, dead. His granddaughter and her daughter had been strangled to death. He could see the red bruise around their necks. They'd been strangled to death. Their eyes bulged, and their mouths were stuck open. Terror was etched across their pale faces.

"Oh, Jesus, no," Hahn let the duffle bag drop to the floor. Instantly, tears filled his eyes and his mouth quivered. His heart ached greatly. He couldn't believe what had occurred, but the evidence was lying before him. "My babies, my sweet, sweet babies…no God, don't let this be happening to me." Still holding his handgun, he crawled over to his granddaughter and her daughter and pulled them into him. Teardrops fell from his eyes as he hugged their lifeless bodies against either side of him. His entire body shuddered as the tears fell from his eyes and splashed on the carpet. Coming down from his grieving, he laid the girls down on their backs and crossed their arms on their chest, making them look like they were lying in coffins. Using his hand, he brushed their eyelids shut and kissed them both on their foreheads affectionately.

Hahn wiped his dripping eyes with his finger. When he looked up from what he was doing he saw something written in red lip stick across the flat-screen's display, *Turn me on and press play.* Hahn frowned because he found this odd. He looked on either side of him until he found the remote control. He picked the remote up and turned on the television. He then activated the DVD player. As soon as he did, he came face to face with Gustavo. When Hahn saw his face, his stomach twisted into knots, and he started feeling nauseated. He thought he was about to throw up. Homie couldn't help the feeling that death was lingering in the air and that made his skin crawl. It also caused his killa instinct to kick in and he gripped his handgun tighter. His trigger finger itched, and he couldn't wait to bust his gun.

"As of right now, I know you're experiencing the same heartache and confusion I was felt when I found Caroline dead."

Gustavo said to him as tears spilled down his cheeks. His eyes were red webbed and glassy. "I don't want chu to make any mistake. I orchestrated this dreadful scene before your eyes. I had the last of your bloodline extinguished so you could feel the pain I feel every day and night." He took the time to pull his handkerchief from the pocket of his suit and dabbed his dripping eyes dry. He then went on to continue. "Tell me, Hahn, do you feel how I feel?" It was silence as Hahn stared at the television screen, tears running down his cheeks. His eyes were pink from crying and his jaws were locked. You could see the bone structure in them. The illumination from the T. V's screen shone on him as he stood before the television holding his gun at his side. A vein pulsated at his temple and his nostrils flared. He started to open fire on the T.V, but he was curious about what else Gustavo had to say, so he stayed his trigger finger. "I thought so. I cannot begin to tell you how good that makes me feel." He smiled. "Your suffering matches my own, but we're not even until you die!" Gustavo smiled wickedly. At that moment, men wearing ski masks and bulletproof vests emerged out of nowhere. They had MP-5s and Glocks.

Noticing some of the ski mask rocking niggaz at the corner of his eye, Hahn brought his handgun up and around. He pulled his trigger and muzzle flashes illuminated his face. A couple of the ski mask wearing niggaz went down when the slugs slammed into their bulletproof vests, but the rest of them opened fire on him. He hollered out in excruciation as automatic gunfire lit his ass up. He managed to get off two more shots, both striking one of his enemies in the head, splattering their blood on the television screen. Turning around, he dropped his handgun and retreated towards the kitchen, catching fire along the way. His blood dotted the floor and the walls as he staggered away from the bullets meant to seal his fate.

Hahn made it inside of the kitchen with bullets flying over his head, hitting the walls he was staggering beside and splintering the kitchen cupboards. Hunched over, he held his hold his bleeding torso, making his way towards the back door of the house. His blood was pelting the kitchen's linoleum, and his vision was blurry. He dropped to his knee, but he pulled himself back upon his feet. As he neared the backdoor, the masked niggaz appeared behind him. Some of them had smoking guns while others were reloading their weapons. One of them went to point his gun to finish Hahn off, but another one of them raised his hand, stopping him. With the order given, the determined shooter lowered his gun to his side. Together, the niggaz in the masks watched as Hahn retreated for his life.

Hahn had gotten ten feet from the backdoor when the last masked gunman appeared. He was carrying a long black shotgun and scowling menacingly. Before Hahn could escape his wrath, homeboy racked his shotgun and let her rip. The first blast spun Hahn around, but the second blew his ass backwards. He went sliding across the floor until he eventually came to a stop at the center of the kitchen floor. Lying on his back, Hahn blinked his eyelids repeatedly and gurgled on his own blood. Blood ran from the corners of his mouth and made small pools on either side of his head. The ski masked men looked down upon him with pity, as he lay beside the stove. They watched as he reached behind the stove, doing God only knew what. They started to smoke him, but they figured he wasn't much of a threat in his condition.

The masked man that blasted on Hahn spat on the floor as he came walking inside of the kitchen, both hands on his smoking shotgun. He could see Hahn's legs sticking out beside the stove as he went around it. He licked his chops and smiled devilishly.

"Ah, there you are." The masked man welding the shotgun said. He found Hahn messing with something behind the stove. Once he kicked him in his side, he howled in pain and rolled over on his back. In one hand, he had a valve that was attached to the back of the stove. Gas escaped from the valve being loose and filled the air. In the other hand, Hahn held a Zippo lighter. Looking to the nigga that had blasted him with the shotgun, he smiled knowingly and struck the small metal ball of his lighter. A bluish yellow flame leaped to life from the lighter. As soon as the flame mingled with the gas in the air, the house exploded and sent fire roaring throughout it. Flames burst out of the windows of the house and sent broken glass out into the night's air. Shards of glass came raining down on the front lawn.

Thud! Thump! Bump!

Burning body parts landed on the front lawn.

Down the block and across the street

Lethal sat behind the wheel of his van watching the raging fire through the windshield. The reflection of Hahn's goddaughter's burning house shone on the windshield. After a minute, he started the van up, pulled out of his parking space and drove off. Gripping the steering wheel with one hand, he pulled his cell phone out of his suit jacket and dialed up Gustavo.

***

After he dropped Big Sexy off at home, Fear drove out to the house he shared with Italia. He parked his motorcycle in the driveway and placed the kickstand down. He then hopped off his bike and hustled up the stairs of his home, pulling out his keys. As he sifted through his keys for the one, he needed to open the front door, he suddenly stopped and listened closely.

His brows furrowed as he waited to hear what he'd heard again, but when he didn't, he shrugged. Thinking nothing of it, Fear opened the door of his house and pushed his way inside. As soon as he crossed the threshold his eyes bulged, and he gasped. Sitting before him was Italia and his mother, Verna, in chairs, gagged and bound. Standing behind them was a man wearing the same face as him, but it wasn't him. It was Malik. His eyes and posture gave him away. Realizing who the man was pointing a silenced gun to the back of Italia's head was, Fear glared up at him and squared his jaws, boasting the bone structure in his face.

"Well, well, well, look who's finally home," Malik smiled sinisterly, like there was a joke that only he knew the punch line to. "You're just in time for the fun and games, Mr. Simpson." He switched hands with the gun and reached inside of his pocket, pulling out a half of a dollar silver coin. "I'm gonna flip this coin, okay? Heads your mom's dies, heads wifey gets it. Ready? Call it in the air." He flipped the coin up in the air and it was flipping so fast that it looked like a silver blur while in motion. It landed in his palm, and he smacked it down on the back of his hand. His head snapped up at Fear and he was smiling harder. "Wutchu got, homie? Heads or Tails?"

"I'm not playing your fucking games!" Fear barked on Malik. He was clenching his fists so tight that veins were running through them. His head shook slightly like it was about to erupt and he was gritting his teeth.

"Wrong! You're gonna play whether you want to or not,

mothafucka! You don't get no choice in the matter." Malik spat at him with a pair of hateful eyes. "Now pick!"

Fear didn't respond. He just stood there mad dogging him.

"I said, 'pick, nigga!'"

There was still no answer.

"Fine! I'ma pick for yo' ass then, you got heads."

"I swear on my father's grave if you harm one hair on either of their heads, I'ma kill yo' ass!"

The man slowly removed his palm from the back of his other hand. Seeing what the verdict was, he smiled sinisterly again and looked up at Fear.

"Well, looks like she can kiss her ass goodbye," he took the silver dollar from his other hand and pointed his weapon at the back of the woman's head that he intended to kill.

"Malik, noooooo!" Fear called out, but it was already too late.

FEAR MY GANGSTA 3

CHAPTER THREE

A white Mercedes-Benz limousine rolled up just outside of an old warehouse that had been shut down for quite some time. It's chauffeur, Lethal, hopped out from behind the wheel and made his way to the back door of the vehicle, opening it up. He stepped aside and Gustavo stepped out. He dropped what was left of his cigar at his feet and mashed it out underneath the heel of his one-thousand-dollar designer leather shoe. He then blew out what was left of the smoke in his lungs and allowed Lethal to slam the door shut behind him. A few seconds later, three of his goons came out of the limousine and joined up with him. A moment later, a black Mercedes-Benz limousine pulled up ahead of them. Its chauffeur hopped out and made his way to the back door of the vehicle, opening its door. Right after, Esteban hopped out and adjusted his cufflinks. A moment later, two of his goons joined either side of him wearing deadly expressions across their faces.

"Mr. Gomez, to what pleasure do I owe this meeting?" Gustavo asked as he extended his hand. Esteban looked at his hand like it was covered in horse manure. He then spit off to the side and licked his lips, looking up at Gustavo as if he hated his fucking guts.

"I've been in this business for over eight years now, and I haven't so much as seen the inside of a holding cell or had the Feds up my ass. The only reason why I started doing business with you was because your prices were cheap, and you have some of the sweetest product I'd ever had the pleasure of coming across." He cleared his throat with his fist to his mouth and continued with what he had to say. "But I must say, I find it very suspect, the moment that I start getting product from you that my shipments are getting hit."

Broli strolled down a line of men at his feet that were lying on their stomachs on the ground. Their mouths were gagged, and their wrists were bound behind their backs with zip-cuffs. They struggled to get free of their restraints, but their efforts were useless. There wasn't any chance in hell they were getting out of their bondages, and even if they did, they'd be cut down by machine gun fire by Broil's men.

"Well, let's take a look at the merchandise, shall we?" Broli said to the men at his mercy. He then switched shoulders with the strap of the compact machine gun he had in his possession. Afterwards, he grabbed hold of the dangling strap on the delivery truck and pulled himself upon the bumper of the vehicle. He unlatched the lock and pulled the shutter of the transporting vehicle open. Inside there were several vases wrapped in cellophane.

Broli grabbed one of the vases and jumped down to the ground. He slammed the vase down and it exploded into pieces. Using his machine gun, Broli rifled through the cellophane and the broken pieces of the vase, until he found a neatly wrapped package. He picked up the package and smiled victoriously, looking around at all his men. "Here we go, boys. The prize we've been looking for."

Some of Broli's men exchanged greedy smiles while others. high fived each other.

"Let's see what we got in this tight lil' package," Broli slung the strap of his machine gun over his shoulder. He then pulled out a big ass hunting knife; it twinkled once the sunlight kissed off it. He then stabbed the package and slit it upwards, spilling cocaine. Broli dabbed his finger into the powdery substance and rubbed it around his gums. Instantly, he felt a numbness surrounding his mouth, like he'd been given a shot of Novocain.

"Just like we thought, boys, co—mothafuckin'—caine...good shit, too."

With that having been said, Broli tossed the opened package into the back of delivery truck beside the rest of the vases. Next, he walked over to the side of the vehicle and picked up a red gas-can. He then locked eyes with his men and gave them a nod. Knowing what he meant by this gesture, the men pointed their machine guns at the men lying bound at his feet and opened fire on them. The restrained men were being massacred; blood and brain fragments were flying everywhere. Some of the blood and brain fragments splattered on the pants legs of the executioners, but they didn't pay it any mind, they kept on firing until all movement among their victims had ceased. Once the men had finished shooting their machine guns wafted with smoke. They ejected the spent cartridges from their automatic weapons and smacked in fresh ones, putting new rounds into the heads of their machine guns.

Broli instructed a couple of the men to drive the trucks back to the location they'd discussed before the lick. He then doused the dead men with gasoline. While he was doing this, the rest of his men were climbing inside of their vehicles and preparing to leave. Broli led a trail of gasoline towards the van he was going to ride shotgun in and dropped the gas-can on the spot. Jumping into the passenger seat, he pulled out his Zippo lighter and sparked up a Newport. He blew out a cloud of smoke and tossed the lighter onto the flammable liquid.

Froosh!

A line of fire ripped up the trail of gasoline and all the dead bodies went up in a burst of flames. Right after, Broli slammed the door shut and signaled for the driver to pull off. The van pulled off while the fire was mingling with the gas-can.

Abruptly, the gas-can exploded and a cloud of fire filled the background of the fleeing van.

"Are you calling me a thief?" Gustavo asked him, eyebrows arched, and nose scrunched up. There were three things on earth that he refused to be called and that was a rat, a coward and/or a thief. To him, all three of them were the lowest forms of life you could be besides a rapist or a child molester.

"If the shoe fits, then buy a purse to match." Esteban stepped closer to Gustavo.

Gustavo hauled off and cracked that mothafucka in the jaw, dropping him. As soon as that punch was thrown, Esteban and Gustavo's men drew their handguns and traded gunfire.

"Ahhhhh, fuck!" Gustavo grabbed his bleeding cheek as a

bullet skinned it. He fell to the ground, and one of his goons helped him to his feet, ushering him back to the limousine. The goon would occasionally stop along the way, turning halfway around and popping shots at the opposition. Once Gustavo was secure inside of the Mercedes-Benz, the goon went back to trading gunfire with Esteban's goons.

One of Gustavo's goons was shot in both of their kneecaps. He hollered out in agony and fell to the ground, dropping his handgun. Right then, on Esteban's orders, one of Esteban's goons grabbed him up and tossed him inside of his boss's limousine. That same goon made sure Esteban was secure inside of the limousine. When he slammed the door shut behind him, he caught a hot one in his neck causing blood to spray out of it. Gritting, he turned around and started shooting at the opposition. While doing this, he caught a few more bullets to the chest and went down a bloody dead mess.

During the gun battle, one of Gustavo's goons took cover behind the Mercedes-Benz, to reload his handgun. As soon as he stood upright, he caught a face full of some hot shit and fell to the ground, his face a bloody, mutilated mess.

Blocka, blocka, blocka, blocka, blocka!

Esteban's remaining goon started retreating back towards his boss's limousine, letting his gun talk tough. He reached inside of his suit and pulled out an identical handgun, letting it join the family business.

Blocka, blocka, blocka, blocka, blocka!

The bullets knocked off the side view mirror, blew several holes through the hood of the Mercedes-Benz and shattered the black tinted window of the vehicle on the driver's side, killing the chauffeur. The driver slumped in the seat, chin touching his chest as blood droplets trickled from the twin holes in his forehead. At that moment, Gustavo had two goons left.

"The chauffeur's down. I'm gonna get 'em out of the driver's seat and get us outta here! You get back to the car and hold the jefe down! You got that?" One of the goons called out to the other goon and he told him 'Okay'.

With the command given, the goon did like he was told, letting his gun go crazy as he retreated towards the Mercedes-Benz.

Pop, pop, pop, pop, pop, pop!

The goon climbed inside of the lengthy vehicle and slammed the door shut. At this time, Gustavo's remaining goon took cover behind the Mercedes-Benz and reloaded his handgun. Stooping low, he made his way back out into the gun battle, letting his gun talk until he made it up to the driver's door. Still firing, he snatched open the driver's door and pulled the dead ass chauffeur out, letting him fall to the ground, bleeding out. Once homeboy was out of the driver's seat, the goon dove inside of the MercedesBenz. Lying across the seats, legs hanging out of the door, he sat his gun down on the floor. He then threw the vehicle in drive and steered it as he held the gas pedal down with his other hand. The Mercedes-Benz sped out of the gun battle, catching gunfire even as it retreated.

Esteban's goon ran after the Mercedes-Benz with his matching handguns. Stopping once he'd gotten so close upon it, he started popping off madly. The bullets from his guns shattered more of the retreating Mercedes-Benz' windshield and put what looked like a thousand more holes into its hood. Seeing that the Mercedes-Benz had gotten too far for him to hit from his distance, the goon lowered his smoking handguns, watching the vehicle grow smaller and smaller the further it got away. Standing there, the goon breathed heavily, his white breath visible in the cool night air. Hearing police car sirens en route to his location, he ran back to Esteban's chauffeur driven limousine, reloading both of his handguns. Once he finished, he stored his handguns inside of the holsters and hopped into the limousine he was driven there in, slamming the door shut. As soon as he did, the chauffeur peeled out of the area, leaving dead bodies, blood, and gun smoke lingering in the air.

***

Fear's eyes shifted from Italia to his mother, Verna, communicating to them what he planned. They understood to the T what he had in mind; they nodded their heads slightly letting him know that they were with it. With his hand down at his side, Fear dropped one finger, then two, then three, fast. When his third finger dropped, Italia and Verna threw themselves aside in their chair.

"...Three!" Malik called out and went to pull the trigger. Before he could pull the trigger, a scowling Fear came off his hip, handgun firing.

Bloc, bloc, bloc!

Malik caught two in his chest and one in his neck. He dropped his gun, and smacked his palm over the hole in the side of his neck that was squirting blood across the air. He went down wincing, collapsing to the carpeted floor. Gripping his banga with both hands, Fear moved in on him cautiously, kicking the gun he was holding out of his reach. His shadow loomed over Malik, as he clutched his neck and stared up at him with blinking eyelids, lips and teeth bloody.

"I'll be back, y'all," Fear looked over his shoulders, telling his

mother and his woman. He ducked off inside of the kitchen and returned with a big ass butcher's knife. *Snikt, snikt!* He removed Verna and Italia restraints, and they pulled off their gags, getting to their feet. They both hugged Fear and thanked him for saving their lives.

Ba-boom!

Splinters flew across the room as the front door was kicked open. Fear jumped in front of the most important women in his life, using himself as a human shield and pointing his gun at the intruder. He found himself standing face to face with Gunplay, they both had their guns trained on one another. Fear and Gunplay mad dogged each other while Verna and Italia exchanged worried glances. They couldn't help wondering what the fuck was about to go down at that moment. The only thing that could be heard was everyone's thudding hearts in their ears. Slowly, Gunplay lowered his gun and pulled his hood off his head, and Fear did the same, tucking his gun at the small of his back.

"My bad for drawing down, big homie, I didn't know what the fuck was going on. I drove by here and I heard gunfire, so I hopped out my shit and kicked the door down. You and yo people good, cuz?" Gunplay asked as he tucked his gun into the front of his jeans and draped the end of his sweatshirt over it.

Fear looked around at his mother and his woman; Verna and Italia were okay. "Yeah, they're straight."

"F—Fear," Malik gurgled on his own blood. Fear walked over to his cousin and kneeled to him. He grabbed the back of his neck and lifted his head up from off the floor, staring into his face and gripping his hand.

"Yeah?" Fear asked, seeing the tears in Malik's eyes and the blood running out of the corners of his mouth, dripping onto the floor.

"I love you, nigga. No—no matter what, I've always loved you." Malik confessed as tears seemed to pour out of his eyes.

"I love you too, reli. Always." Fear told him with a stone face and tears in his eyes. He didn't want to murk his cousin, but the nigga didn't really leave him a choice. He had to do what he had to do to save his mother and the woman he loved.

Malik's eyes looked down at the gun Fear hand in his hand, he grabbed his cousin by the hand that he held the gun with and brought it to his chest, where his heart was. "Finish—" Malik squeezed his eyelids shut as he gagged and coughed up blood. "Finish it. Fin—finish it, please."

"A.J.," Verna called out to her son, tears rolling down her cheeks. Fear looked over his shoulder at his mother. "Don't, son.

Don't do it." She wiped away her dripping tears with her curled finger.

"It's—it's okay, aunt—auntie." Malik said to the woman that had wed his uncle Alvin. He cracked a half smile at her, and she smirked at him. She then buried her face into Italia's bosom and

cried her eyes out as the young girl comforted her.

Gunplay stood aside, watching everything that was taking place. He was a little taken aback seeing Fear about to kill someone who mirrored his image. He was sure he had a perfect explanation of who the nigga was he was holding in his arms, begging for a mercy killing.

"Go go ahead, Blood." Malik told Fear.

Fear looked his cousin straight into his eyes and pulled the trigger, killing him instantly. The tension released from Malik's body, and he took his last breath, going stiff in Fear's arms.

Once Fear had put Malik out of his misery, he motioned Gunplay over with the hand he was holding his handgun with. Together, they moved all the furniture from the center of the living room and rolled Malik's body up inside of the floor rug, snuggly. Afterwards, Verna approached Fear crying her eyes out, and he hugged her, kissing her on top of her head.

"I wanna know. I wanna know where your father and I went wrong for you to lead the life that you have now. Please, tell me." She looked up at him as tears continued to pour down her face.

Fear wiped her tears away with his fingers and thumb.

"You and pop were strict, but it didn't lead me down this road. This was always the life I wanted. I don't know why exactly, and excuse my language when I say this, but this—this gangsta shit is in me. The streets were calling, and I answered." Fear gave his mother the raw and uncut truth. Upon hearing it, she broke down sobbing and crying again, planting her face into his chest. He hugged her tightly and comforted her as best as he could.

"Yo, is that nigga we rolled up yo brotha?"

"Nah," Fear shook his head. "*That* brother's my relative. My cousin. I believe he got plastic surgery to get the same face as mine. The suicide of his brother and spending all that time behind concrete and steel musta really screwed up his mind. Drove 'em insane. It led him to get plastic surgery so that he could have the same face as mine." He went on to give Gunplay the rundown on him and his twin cousins Malik and Wameek. He also told him why he gave up the crack game and what game he was focused on now that he was home. "I'ma needa favor from you, family." He told Gunplay.

"Speak on it, big dawg." Gunplay folded his arms across his chest and waited to hear what he had to say.

"I need you to bury my loved one while I get my mom's and my lady on the next thing outta here."

"Wait a minute," Italia interjected. "I'm not going anywhere.

I'm staying here witchu. Whatever you're involved in we'll be facing it together."

"Baby, I'm just tryna make sure that you and momma are…"

Italia cut him short by placing her finger to his lips, saying, "Save it, tiger. I'm not taking no for an answer. You've got cho self a ride or die."

Fear stared into her eyes for a moment, trying to see if she was fronting. She wasn't so he decided to let her ride it out with him. "Alright, lil' mama, you staying then."

"Alright, bro, I got chu faded. Just help me get 'em into the trunk." Gunplay told Fear.

"Swang yo whip around into the alley, at the back of the house, we'll put 'em in out there, my nigga. I'm not tryna have this entire hood in mine, you Griff me?" "I got chu." He nodded.

"Good looking out." Fear held out his fist.

"No doubt," Gunplay touched fists with him and hurried outside. He swung his car around the alley and called Fear to come outside. Together, they dumped Malik inside of the trunk and dapped up.

"Bang my line once you handle that, so I'll know you straight." Fear told Gunplay.

"Fa sho," Gunplay jumped back behind the wheel of his car and slammed the door shut, pulling off down the alley. Fear watched the back of his vehicle until its red brake lights disappeared into the night. Afterwards, he hustled back inside of the house and got his mother and his fiancée. They dipped out to Calabasas to his parents' house where his mother packed her luggage. Then, they headed out to the Greyhound station so Verna could catch a bus to Connecticut where a lot of their family lived.

***

Verna pulled up inside of the transportation depot and killed the engine of the vehicle. Her, Verna and Fear jumped out of the car and mobbed up to the Greyhound station, by passing people that were coming and going. As soon as they crossed the threshold, they were met with a mesh of voices of people conversing. Fear gave his mother the money to purchase her ticket to Connecticut, while he and Italia got a few things out of vending machines.

Verna copped her ticket from the window and met back up with her son and his fiancée.

"Ma, when is the bus arriving?" Fear asked his mother as he cracked open a can of Coca Cola.

Verna glanced at her watch and said, "An hour from now."

"Well, we've got plenty of time to chat before you leave, let's finda place to sit and chat." Italia said, looking around for a place for all of them to sit. Once she discovered one, she motioned for all of them to follow her and they sat down.

***

After disposing of Malik's body for Fear, Gunplay checked in with him to let him know that he was good. Afterwards, he went home to shower and change his clothing. Thereafter, he found himself at the liquor store. Gunplay paid for his items, took his change and grabbed his black plastic bag of goods. Turning around, he stuck his straw of licorice into his mouth and headed for the exit. A bell dinged as he crossed the threshold coming out of the store. Making his way down the street, he saw a homeless man posted up on the side of the liquor store. He was rattling a McDonald's cup of change and wearing a cardboard sign around his neck which read: Homeless. Hungry. Please, help! The man was rocking a baseball cap and a navy-blue hoodie which was underneath a hefty brown trench coat. The bearded man's head was on a swivel, taking in his surroundings, looking for anyone that would possibly bless him with a little something to get something to eat.

Gunplay spotted the homeless man and decided to bless him with a little something, something. Stopping before him, he switched hands with the black bag and reached inside his pocket. He pulled out the couple of dollars and the loose change he'd gotten from his purchase.

"Here you go, my ni—" Gunplay's eyes widen with surprise when he came face to face with a black handgun. His eyes looked to the face of the man behind the trigger. He was scowling and clenching his jaws. "Cuz, what the fuck is this?"

"A Glock 40!" The homeless man told him. He then smacked the money out of his hands. The dollars and the loose change pinged off the curb. "Gemme that goddamn licorice, nigga!" He snatched the red candy straw from out of his mouth and stuck it into his. He then grabbed his bag and threw it to the sidewalk. Afterwards, he looked up and down the block to make sure there wasn't anyone watching. Seeing that there wasn't anybody watching him, he ushered Gunplay into the liquor store's parking lot at gunpoint.

"My nigga, what the fuck is this about?" Gunplay asked,

looking at the man from the corner of his eyes.

"My boy, if you open yo' dicksuckas one mo' time, I'ma put a bullet between 'em! My right hand to The Most High. Stop right here." The homeless man stopped Gunplay at the hood of his Charger and told him to place his hands on it. He then pulled out a pair of handcuffs. Keeping his banga at the back of his dome piece, he went on to lock the metal bracelets around his wrists. "Okay, now let's get cho ass into the backseat of my ride."

Once the homeless man placed Gunplay into the backseat of his Charger, he slammed the door shut behind him and jumped in behind the wheel. He sat his tool down on the front passenger seat. Looking up into the rearview mirror, he removed his cap and the bushy mustache and beard. It was Broli. He placed his disguise into the glove-box and smacked it closed.

Broli fired up his Charged and pulled out of the parking lot. As he cruised through the streets, he glanced up into the rearview mirror. He spotted Gunplay looking around in the backseat for a means to escape.

"Alright, lil' nigga," Broli began. "I know I'm driving yo' young ass crazy wondering what I plan on doing witchu, so let's get to it. You know who I am?" He glanced into the backseat so Gunplay could get a good look at him.

There was silence, but Broli saw the look of recognition on the young nigga'z face.

"Well, you remember me?" Broli inquired. Gunplay shrugged.

"Nigga, I asked you a mothafucking question. I suggest yo' ass answer." he frowned up, nostrils flaring with attitude.

"Mothafucka, you told me the next time I opened my mouth; you were gonna put a bullet in it. So, excuse the fuck outta me if I'm not so quick to answer yo' police-ass." Gunplay responded with slanted eyebrows.

"Well, now I'm granting you permission, nigga!"

"Yeah, I know who you are," he confirmed. "You that crooked badge Sex had me drop that footage off to."

Broli nodded and said, "Your memory serves you correct. Now, I'm sure the big man told you I was blackmailing him for a bag every week or so, but I bet he didn't tell you what I was blackmailing 'em with, now did he?"

Gunplay frowned up. "I figured you were blackmailing 'em with the fact that you were One Time, and you knew how he was getting to the paypa."

"Nahhhh," he shook his head. "That's not how I was working my angle, homeboy." He grabbed the file tucked between the console and his seat, wagging it before Gunplay's eyes.

"What's that?"

"I'ma 'bouta show you." Broli sat the file down on the

passenger seat. He then pulled over into a dark alley and turned on the dome light. Grabbing his gun and the file, he jumped out of his car. He opened the backdoor and slid in beside Gunplay. "By the time you finish reading through this paperwork, I bet cho feelings about cho man change."

Switching hands with the gun, Broli opened the file and showed the first document to Gunplay. He allowed him to read everything that had been reported to him by Broli. Once the young nigga finished reading the document, Broli let him read the next one and then the next one. The crooked badge went through the file until Gunplay had read through everything. By the time he finished, Broli could tell that his mind was blown by the paperwork.

Gunplay shut his eyelids and dropped his head back against the seat. "How I know this shit real? The fuck I know you didn't make all this shit up you showing me?" He peeled his eyelids back open and looked at Broli. "I know how you mothafucking pigs get down, y'all some crafty ass mothafuckaz. Y'all not to be trusted."

"Youngsta, believe whatever the fuck you wanna believe. I don't give two shits. I'm just giving you fair warning," Broli told him as he pulled him out of the back of his Charger, placing his stomach against the side of it. He then pulled out his handcuff key to unlock the metal bracelets from around his wrists. "Know this though. Once the shit hits the fan, and y'all lil' crack empire folds, don't say no one ever gave you a heads up on how yo' people get down." he removed the handcuffs from Gunplay's wrists. The young nigga turned around to him, rubbing his sore wrists. "Here you go. That's all you." He handed him the file and he took it. "I gotta million copies of that. If I were you, I'd get that out to all my homeboys so they'll know what's up."

Once he'd given Gunplay the file, Broli jumped in behind the wheel of his Charger and pulled out of the alley. Driving in reverse, he glanced through the windshield seeing Gunplay flip through the pages of the file again. A slight smirk formed on his lips knowing that the young nigga was going to do exactly what he wanted him to do, or so he hoped.

CHAPTER FOUR

It had been a couple of days since Fear had heard from Hahn, so he decided to holla at him. He pulled out his cellular and hit him up. His phone call went straight to voicemail, so he called again, again and again, getting the same response. Having grown frustrated, he tossed his cell phone aside and fired up his vehicle, programming his destination into his GPS. An hour later he and Italia was pulling up at his destination and he was hopping out of the car, making his way toward the double glass doors of Hahn's dojo, which had dragons circling themselves on either door, with the name of the dojo in Japanese letters.

Fear pressed his face and hands against the glass door, looking around the dark dojo. He held down the button of the intercom and spoke loud enough for anyone that maybe listening to hear him. He did this three times but didn't receive an answer. That's when he pulled two pins from out of the small pocket above his big pocket and picked the lock to the doors of the dojo. Once the doors popped open, Fear looked over his shoulders to see if he was being watched. He wasn't. So he made his way inside of the dark dojo, closing the door behind him, looking around the dark establishment. His eyes took in the trophies that were behind the display glass, portraits of students of Master Hahn's dojo lining the wall, and practice dummies.

Fear peeked outside at the greenhouse where all of the plants and trees that Master Hahn had grown were. Once he didn't see anyone out in the greenhouse, he made his way back inside of the dojo and up the stairs to Master Hahn's bedroom door. Fear was about to pick the lock of the bedroom door, when he smelled gas escaping from underneath the door. His brows furrowed and he wondered what was going on. Fear's curiosity got the best of him, and he went ahead with picking the lock of the bedroom door but found that it was already unlocked. As soon as he opened the door, he found a masked-up nigga dousing the bedroom's bed and furniture with gasoline, from a red can.

"Who the fuck are you? And where is Master Hahn?" Fear's forehead crinkled and he pulled out his handgun.

"Dead. Like you're about to be," A masked up Lethal proclaimed and tossed the red gas can aside. As soon as Fear went to point his handgun at the masked intruder, Lethal threw a ninja star at his ass. It spun so fast at him that it became a silver blur. The deadly weapon knocked the handgun out of Fear's hand just as he pulled the trigger, and it fired. As soon as that happened, Lethal moved in and they locked ass. They blocked one another's moves and countered, trying to land a fatal blow that would end each other's lives.

Bwap, wap, wop, crack!

Fear landed four devastating blows that staggered Lethal. He then got back into a martial art fighting stance, motioning for him to come forward for some more. Lethal rushed at him, moving so fast that the human eye couldn't detect the punches and kicks he threw. Fear managed to see them all though, and he blocked all of his attacks effortlessly. Lethal drew back, following up with a punch to Fear's gut and then two kicks to his head, knocking sweat from off him. From there, Fear was in trouble, taking hit after hit, unable to block any more of Lethal's attacks. A blow to the midsection dropped him down to his knees, leaving him holding his stomach, breathing hard. Fear looked up, seeing Lethal poised to make a kill-strike. The Asian man's fingers were the shape of claws. He was going to attempt to rip Fear's heart out of his chest.

"Yaaa!" Lethal called out and drove his hand forward. At the last minute, Fear did a back flip out of the way to avoid being assaulted. He scanned the floor hastily until he found what he was looking for. The red gas can. He grabbed the gas can and threw it towards Lethal. He then snatched up his handgun and aimed it at the gas can, pulling the trigger. Sparks flew out of the gun as it fired a bullet. The bullet came out of the gun in what looked like slow motion. The bullet struck the gas can and it ignited, exploded into flames. The impact from the blast sent Lethal hurling backwards and going through the window, shattering the glass. He hollered as he plummeted to the ground below.

Fear lowered his handgun and slowly approached the window, which was on fire now. Once he reached the window, he peered over and out of it, seeing Lethal slowly getting up from off the sidewalk. He limped away holding the lower half of his back. Peering closely, Fear could see the large tear in Lethal's black thermal. It revealed a dragon blowing fire.

Fear aimed his gun at a fleeing Lethal but he couldn't draw a bead on him, so he hurried down the staircase to try to catch him. He kicked open the double doors of Master Hahn's dojo and ran outside, gripping his handgun at his side. His head looked up and down the block for his assailant, but he didn't see him. It wasn't until he heard a car's tires squealing that he looked to his left. When he did, he saw a Mercedes-Benz van bending the corner with Lethal in it, heading off in the opposite direction. Fear ran into the street, then chased the van several blocks, running up on cars and jumping from rooftop to rooftop. Once he figured he'd gotten close enough to take a shot at the van, he jumped down into the street and aimed his gun at the back of the fleeing vehicle. He pulled the trigger back-to-back, spitting flames at it.

Bloc, bloc, bloc, bloc, bloc!

Fear's rapid gunplay shattered the back windows of the Mercedes-Benz and caused it to swerve out of control, nearly crashing before its driver regained control of the vehicle and kept it on the street.

"Damn, fuck!" Fear cussed and swung on the air he was so pissed off. He then tucked his handgun into the small of his back, fleeing back to his vehicle. He jumped into his car and Italia pulled off, just as he heard police sirens wailing in the distance. A second later, he got a call from someone down at the morgue telling him to come identify a body. Right then, his heart dropped because something told him it was Master Hahn's dead body he was going to see.

***

Lethal sped through the streets wincing, glancing back and forth over his shoulder. He could see Fear growing smaller and smaller behind him. Seeing that there wasn't any way that Fear was going to catch up with him, Lethal looked at his arm, he had two bullets in his shit, and they were burning like hell. Pulling out his cell phone, he hit up Gustavo and told him to have his doctor friend come to the mansion. When the kingpin asked him what happened, he told him he'd holler at him once he got there.

Gustavo had sent Lethal to burn down Master Hahn's dojo. The kingpin passed the dojo every morning to get breakfast at his favorite diner. Every time he would see the dojo it would piss him off. So, he decided to have Lethal burn that bitch down to the ground. He wanted any and everything that had to do with Master Hahn to be destroyed.

Lethal sat his cellular down on the holder attached to the dashboard. Glancing back up, he saw the tattoo above his right eyebrow: *Loyalty*. He touched the ink like it wasn't a part of his face and remembered that he'd gotten it in honor of Gustavo. He got it as a reminder to always be loyal to him because he was the man that had taken him out of the streets.

A thirty-two-year-old Gustavo walked inside of Waleeto's pizza parlor. He waltzed right up to the counter and ordered himself two slices of cheese pizza and a pink lemonade Hi-C which he paid for with a fifty-dollar bill. The cashier, Mr. Waleeto, an older gentleman rocking a plaid shirt and white pasta-stained apron, rung up his order and gave him his change. Mr. Waleeto then called out to his son, Junior, who was inside of the kitchen, to make one large cheese pizza.

"Alright, pop." Junior replied as he pounded the pizza dough with his bare hands and then flattened it out with a rolling pin.

"Thank you." Mr. Waleeto told Gustavo as he dropped his

change from his meal inside of the clear glass jar labeled Tips.

"Don't mention it." Gustavo patted Mr. Waleeto on the cheek and pinched it like he was some sort of fucking mob figure before walking over to his table with his beverage. Waleeto cracked a smile, but it dropped from his face once Gustavo turned to walk away. He hated when that nigga patted his cheek and pinched it like he was a little kid. He was a fifty-seven-year-old grown man. The only reason he didn't say anything was because he knew Gustavo rolled with them boys that played with those guns. And he wasn't one to indulge in gangsta activities, nor was he friends with anyone that did.

Seeing that the kitchen floor needed to be swept, Mr. Waleeto left and returned with a broom to get right down to business. While he was doing his duty, Gustavo was sliding a straw into his beverage and watching the basketball game on the square, boxed television set mounted high upon the wall. He was so engrossed in the game that he didn't see an eighteen-year-old Lethal, who was dressed in shabby clothing and beat up sneakers, creep inside of the parlor. The kid saw that everyone inside of the parlor was busy with something, so he knew it was the perfect time for him to try to steal something to eat. Lethal's stomach had been growling and he was starving.

Lethal hunched over and made hurried footsteps towards the counter, stopping right underneath a short rack of chips. He looked at Gustavo to make sure he wasn't watching him, and he wasn't. Acknowledging this, Lethal stood upright and picked up the entire rack of chips, tip toeing towards the door. He'd gotten halfway there when he heard Mr. Waleeto's voice which called an ice sickle to slide down his back and his hairs to stand up on his neck.

"Where do you think you're going, you liddle shit?" Mr.

Waleeto ran over to the door of the parlor and locked it. He had an angry expression fixed on his face and a broom in his hand, gripping it so tightly that veins bulged in his hands.

The moment Gustavo heard Mr. Waleeto's voice he looked over his shoulder. He started to stop what he knew was going to occur. But his curiosity had gotten the best of him, and he decided to watch the show.

"Oh, fuck!" Lethal said when he saw Mr. Waleeto. His eyes got big as shit and his jaw dropped. He then hoisted up the rack and threw it at his ass. Mr. Waleeto dodged the flying chip rack and it slammed into one of the large windows of the parlor, cracking its glass into a spider's cobweb.

"Oh, that's your ass, boy!" Mr. Waleeto charged at Lethal swinging the broom wildly. The broom whistled as it swung through the air. The old man went at Lethal's head, body and legs, all of which the boy dodged with ease. Mr. Waleeto then swung the broom stick downward, Lethal side stepped it and it slammed into the floor. Lethal kicked him in the back of his kneecap which dropped him down to one knee and then he gave him a round house kick to the head, dropping his old ass.

"Aaaahhhhh!" A battle cry came from behind Lethal. He looked over his shoulder and saw Mr. Waleeto's son, Junior, charging at him with a fucking meat cleaver. The youngsta swung that blade fast and hard. He was trying to make minced meat out of Lethal. But the boy was just to goddamn quick on his feet to be scathed by the meat cleaver. When Junior swung the meat cleaver for Lethal's neck, he caught the young man by his wrist and twisted his arm. A sharp pain shot through the youngsta's arm, and he dropped the meat cleaver. It clinked to the surface. Still holding that same arm, Lethal then jumped up into the air and brought his right leg down on Junior's back. The impact from Lethal fall slammed Junior's face into the table, breaking it and bloodying his nose.

Lethal ran over to the chip rack and stuffed his shirt full of potato chips. He unlocked the door and was about to run up out of that bitch until he heard the metal hammer of a revolver cocking back. The sound of death at the boy's back made him stop in his tracks and lift his hands high into the air. His eyes widen and he swallowed the ball of fear in his throat when he turned around and saw old man Waleeto. The old nigga was leaned over the counter, bleeding at the corner of his mouth, a .44 Magnum revolver pointed at him. He could tell by the mad dog expression written across his face that he'd blow him out of his raggedy ass sneakers if he made another move towards the door of the parlor.

"Kiss your ass goodbye, boy!" Waleeto gritted his teeth and went to pull the trigger of his pistol until Gustavo walked into his path, shielding him from Lethal. Waleeto's face balled up with confusion, wondering why the nigga had stepped into the path of the bullet he was about to cast.

"That's enough, the kids with me." Gustavo told him and pulled some money out of his pocket. He peeled off twenty-onehundred-dollar bills and sat them on the counter, placing a parmesan cheese shaker on top of it. "That should cover the damages here and your kid's emergency room visit." He looked at Lethal. "Aye, kid, how about a couple of slices of pizza?"

Lethal didn't say anything for a while. He couldn't believe the man had stepped in and saved his skinny ass. He blinked his eyelids twice and then he responded. "Yeah, can I get pepperoni?"

"Sure. What do ya want to drink with that?"

"A Coke, please."

"You've got it, Short Round," Gustavo dropped a few more bucks on the counter. "Give the kids three slices of pepperoni pizza and a large Coke, okay?"

Mr. Waleeto nodded and put his gun behind the counter where he'd drawn it from. He then gathered up the money and stacked it neatly. He was a greedy bastard that loved money. He wasn't going to fix the breakage in the window or pay for his son's ER visit. Hell, he wasn't going to take him for that matter. Fuck that!

He was going to stash that money with the rest of the money he had stashed.

Mr. Waleeto licked his thumb and counted the money. Satisfied with what he'd been compensated with, he folded the wad up and stuffed it inside of his pocket. His son approached him from behind holding an ice pack to the back of his head, wincing. He turned to him and said, "Junior, make a large pepperoni pizza."

"Yes, pop, coming right up." Junior turned around and headed back inside of the kitchen to do what he had been told.

"Can I call my girlfriend in, please? She's hungry, too. You don't have to buy here a slice; she'll share with me." Lethal told him.

"Nah, she'll have her own food, too." Gustavo looked over his shoulder and told Mr. Waleeto to make it six slices of pepperoni pizza. Mr. Waleeto told him 'Okay' and relayed the message to his son.

Lethal left the parlor and came back with a blonde hair, blue eyed white girl just as shabbily dressed as he was. She had on a dingy yellow sundress and graying Air Force Ones that were once white. She seemed to find it hard to make eye contact with Gustavo no matter what. Still, Gustavo talked to her and Lethal as they ate their slices of pizza. As they ate, Gustavo found out a lot of things about Lethal. For instance, he was an orphan and he met Vanessa, the white girl, in foster care. They ran away because they were being molested and sexually abused. They'd been running the streets for the past four years together stealing and eating out of trash cans to get by. Gustavo also found out that Lethal learned Karate from his first foster daddy who was shot and killed during a home invasion. He taught the kid a lot about being a man and how to defend himself.

"Tell me, Lethal, have you ever killed anyone before?" Gustavo asked him, wiping his mouth with a napkin and then balling it up, dropping it into the paper plate he was given the pizza slices on.

Lethal scoffed down the last of his pizza and washed it down with Coke. His mouth was greasy when he responded. "No. I've never killed anyone before."

"Do you think you could do it if you were being paid?"

"I'm sure I could, especially if it were to take me and my girl outta our situation."

"Good, good," Gustavo sucked the last of his soda from his straw and sat the cup down on the tabletop.

Gustavo, Lethal and Vanessa cruised throughout the city in his dropped top Jaguar, taking in the sights of the city and listening to the Beach Boys. Gustavo took them shopping for clothing, cell phones, other electronics and then he took them out to eat again. Once night fell on the City of Angels (Los Angeles), Gustavo took the top off his fancy ride and lit up a joint, sharing it with Lethal since Vanessa had fallen asleep across the backseat. The fellas got good and high, and started chopping it up some.

"Sooooo, about what we talked about back there at the pizza parlor. How much would it take for you to kill someone?" Gustavo glanced back and forth between the windshield and Lethal.

Lethal took the time to think about it, massaging his chin and staring out of the corners of his eyes. Coming up with the price he'd want to split a nigga'z wig, he turned around to

Gustavo and said, "Ten thousand. Ten thousand dollars is what I'd want to pop someone."

"That's peanuts compared to what you'd get working with me."

He had Lethal's interest now. Gustavo dressed in nice clothes, drove a luxury car and spent money like it was raining from out of the sky. So, he was interested in what he did for a living. "What is it that you do for a living?"

Gustavo smiled at him and said, "It's getting chili out here, lemme put the top back up." He pressed the button that brought the hard top back upon his Jaguar. He then told Lethal that he was the neighborhood dopeman, but he was looking to expand so he was going to need a hitta on his team. A mothafucka that didn't mind killing when people didn't kick in what they owed or violated him.

"I'm hoping that I can find that within you. I really do, because I really like you, kid." Gustavo told him, taking a few hits from the joint and then blowing out smoke. He then dabbed out the ember of the joint inside of his vehicle's ashtray. "So, do you think you got it in you to be my numbre uno enforcer?" A serious-faced Lethal nodded. "Good, very good. Open that glove box there. There's something in there for you." Lethal popped the glove box open and a .9mm Taurus handgun was inside along with stacks of money. A 'wow' look was on Lethal's face as he examined the handgun and sat it in his lap. He then took out the stacks of money and tried to guess how much it was.

"This has got to be like, fifteen, twenty thousand here." He guessed, holding three stacks in one hand and two stacks in the other, an amazed expression written across his face.

"That's twenty-five grand, my friend. You'll be making twentyfive grand for each man you kill for me. As a matter of fact, you're gonna earn what chu got in your hand there right now." Gustavo pulled over to the side of the curb and killed the engine and headlights. He then grabbed the stacks of money from Lethal and tossed them inside of the glove box, slamming it shut. The only thing that Lethal had now was the .9mm Taurus. "Alright, kid, the fun and games are over. Are you ready to earn that twenty-five grand in the glove box or what?"

Lethal looked in the backseat at his sleeping girlfriend, Vanessa. He knew that if he turned down Gustavo's offer it would result in them going back to the streets. And he wasn't having that. It was way too hard being in the streets how they were. The way he saw it, he'd kill whoever Gustavo wanted him to and ten more mothafuckaz that looked just like them, if it meant he didn't have to stay within the concrete jungle.

"Come on, kid, I don't have all day." Gustavo told him, getting antsy.

"Fuck it. I'm down with it." Lethal assured him.

"Good," Gustavo smiled and patted him on the back. "The way you handled old man Waleeto and his son Junior, I knew then that I wanted your talents on my side. Now, all you gotta do is pop someone of my choosing and you're in, kid. Sound simple enough?"

He nodded and said, "Who do you have in mind? Someone you're beefing with over drug territory? Some thieving bastard ran off and didn't pay you? Whomever it is that's gotta problem with you has a problem with me."

"I'm glad to hear that, kid. But it's not gonna be that easy. The guy I want chu to pop is a regular old Joe. A civilian without any street ties, you follow me?"

A surprised look came over Lethal's face. He was okay with popping somebody that was within the street life, but he wasn't quite sure how he felt about killing someone that was innocent. Just then, he glanced into the backseat at Vanessa, and seeing how peaceful she was sleeping, he knew he didn't want to disrupt that and go back to sleeping in tints and eating out of the trash bins in the alleys of restaurants downtown again.

"What's the problem, junior? You changed your mind?"

Gustavo asked, creases in his brows.

"Nah, I'm good to go."

"Alright then. Let's just wait. I'm sure our victim will come strolling out in no time."

Gustavo and Lethal focused their attention off the windshield at a house. An old African American man came strolling out with a cane and a big ass 40-ounce bottle of Olde English malt liquor. He stopped just outside of the yard of the house and guzzled the 40 a third down. He then twisted the cap back on it and sat it down beside him. Next, he pulled out a loose cigarette from his breast pocket and placed it inside of his mouth. Cupping his hand around it as he lit it up with a Bic lighter, allowing its blue flame to lick its tip until it turned ember. He then blew out a cloud of smoke and watched the night, enjoying his cancer stick.

Lethal plucked the half smoked joint from out of the ashtray and stuck it out of the window, waving it at the old man, saying,

"Yo, chief, you gotta light?"

The old man looked around trying to see where the voice was coming from. He couldn't quite see being that it was night, and his vision was already declining with his old age, so he pulled out his glasses and slid them onto his face.

"Oh, there you are. Yeah, I've gotta light. I'll be right over."

The old man told Lethal and stuck the cigarette into his mouth. He then switched hands with his cane and made his way over to the Jaguar, pulling his lighter back out while in motion. He leaned down into the passenger door's window and met Lethal's .9mm Taurus. The cigarette dropped from out of the old man's mouth and his eyes got as big as saucers.

"Oh, Jesus, help me, Father..." the old man uttered before the top of his skull was blown off. Blood, bone, and brain fragments flew everywhere. The old dude dropped to the curb, staring out a pair of lifeless eyes.

Vrooooom!

Gustavo sped off before the old man even hit the ground.

Lethal and Gustavo would go on to develop a father and son relationship. Blood couldn't bring them any closer. Lethal killed many people on Gustavo's behalf. Murder wasn't anything to the young Japanese kid, but nothing could prepare him for the day he'd have to take out the love of his life. You see, while Lethal was out handling business for Gustavo, Vanessa became a high maintenance party girl, hanging with celebrities and rich folk. One day she got pulled over by the police and hauled down to the station for possession of over an ounce of cocaine. She wasn't selling the shit; she was using it. She'd become a cokehead thanks to her frequently attending star studded party events. Anyway, a detective, one that had it bad for Gustavo, spooked her into wearing a wire to try to get evidence on

Gustavo and Lethal. She agreed to it, but only if she were provided witness protection and her fiancé, Lethal, would get full immunity for his involvement.

Vanessa stood in the bathroom mirror with her fully made-up face on, getting ready for a dinner party at Gustavo's mansion. She was in a white bra and panties, trying to tape a wire onto her body. Suddenly, the bathroom door swung open and Lethal stepped in, with his tie loosely around his neck, dressed in a suit.

"Baby, can you tie this for me, pl—" Lethal's words died in his throat seeing that the love of his life was putting on a wire. "What the fuck are you doing?"

"I, uh, I—" Vanessa stammered, at a loss for words. Lethal stormed over to her and turned her around, seeing that the wire led to a tape recorder. She yelped as he snatched the wire that was taped to her torso from her body. He examined it and then threw it to the floor.

"Do you know what you've done, Vanessa? Do you know what position you've put me in?" Lethal grabbed her by her neck with both hands and forced her up against the wall, staring into her eyes, madness dancing in his pupils. Tears pooled in his eyes and dripped off the brims of them. "I loved you! I would have done anything for you, and you betrayed my trust! Gustavo will kill us both when he finds out! Do you understand? He will kill us both!"

"I know, I know, I know, honey, and I'm sorry. I'm so, so sorry!" Vanessa broke down sobbing, tears flooding her face causing her makeup to run. She trembled all over, fearful of what was going to happen next. Surprisingly, Lethal hugged her and cried his eyes out. In fact, they both cried their eyes out while in one another's arms. He then shoved her away from him and pulled his gun out from the small of his back, pointing it at her. "Baby, pleaseeeee!"

Blowl!

A bullet ripped through her stomach, and she touched the place it had entered, fingertips coming away bloody, she held her hand before her eyes. She looked up at Lethal and he was aiming his gun at her forehead. He looked away as he pulled the trigger, blowing her brain against the shower curtains. Vanessa fell backwards inside of the tub, her blood running down into the drain. After the deed was done, Lethal licked his thumb and swept it above his right eyebrow, revealing the loyalty tattoo he'd covered up with makeup. In doing this, he remembered the vow he made to Gustavo to always be loyal to him. With that in mind, he picked up his cell phone and called Gustavo. He arrived shortly. The kingpin hugged him and kissed him on the side of his face, rubbing his back soothingly, listening to him cry.

"There, there, there, it's okay, kid. You did the right thing."

Gustavo told him. He then hit up his cleanup crew and they came by to get rid of Vanessa's dead body.

Having to murder Vanessa was something Lethal would never get over. Although she turned out to be a rat that could have had him, Gustavo, and all his acquaintances locked up for years, it didn't change the fact that he loved her with all his heart. After her death, he became more brutal and cold-hearted. It was something he couldn't help.

Glancing back up at the rearview mirror, Lethal saw tears trickling down his cheeks. He quickly wiped them away with the sleeve of his shirt and continued to mash out through the streets.

***

"Aaaaaaaah fuck!" Lethal cried out and then took a bottle of Jack Daniels to the head, guzzling it. As he thirstily drunk from the bottle, his throat rolled up and down his neck. Now he was inside one of the bathrooms of Gustavo's mansion, with a white balding doctor that had a neck like a fucking buzzard. The doctor was in green scrubs and digging into Lethal's back with medical instruments, trying to get the metal slugs out that he'd been hit with when Fear blasted on his ass. Gustavo stood in the doorway, watching the entire scene before his eyes with his arms folded across his chest, illegal Cuban cigar wedged between his fingers. Smoke wafted all around him as he took casual pulls from the overgrown cancer stick.

"Raaaaaah, fuck, fuck, shit, fuck…" Lethal cried aloud, spittle flying from off his lips as he looked over his shoulder at the doctor. The M.D.'s face was masked with concentration as he skillfully dug out of one of the slugs in his arm. "Gaahhhh, fuck me!"

"Jesus, you cuss more than a god damn sailor! I almost got the first one, so see if you can hack it until we get 'em all out." The good doctor told him.

Lethal turned up the bottle of Jack, guzzling it again, trying to get drunk so he wouldn't feel the pain of the doctor digging in his limb.

"Got it!" The doctor smiled having pulled the first slug out of Lethal. Using the medical instrument, he held up the copper, blood-stained bullet, smiling at it behind the surgical mask that he was wearing. Lethal looked over his shoulder at the bullet that the doctor was holding, wincing. "So, this is the little copper brown bitch that's been a pain in your ass, huh?" He dumped the slug into the tin bowl and fished out the other one as well, dropping it inside of the tin bowl also. He then went about the task of dressing up the wounds and patching them up.

Once the good doctor was done, he gave Lethal some pain killaz and packed up his shit. Gustavo gave him a fat ass stack of dead white men and sent him on his way, patting him on his back as he made his way out of the front door.

"Now, tell me what happened back there." Gustavo told Lethal.

"Well, I went over there to burn that fucking place to the ground, and while I was dousing the joint with gasoline, you won't believe who shows up."

"Who?" Gustavo asked curiously, wondering who it was that Lethal seen at the dojo.

"Fear, Al or whatever the fuck you wanna call 'em." He took the Jack bottle to the head again.

"Interesting. What the hell was he doing there?"

"From what I gathered from portraits there, the old man trained 'em. And if that's so he made 'em a lethal weapon 'cause that bastard can throw hands. One of the meanest sons of bitchez I ever got down with, but I'd like to think I held my own against 'em…" Lethal went on to tell Gustavo everything else that had happened earlier that night.

"From now on I want chu on 'em like stink on shit. I wanna know his every fucking move." He told him. "For all I know this connection with Hahn is more than just a teacher student relationship, it could be something more serious. But if it's not I'll leave it alone, but I've gotta be sure first."

Lethal nodded and continued to guzzle the Jack.

***

Fear and Italia made their way through the morgue, hand and hand. The place was cold and quiet, and they could feel death surrounding them. They took in the place in its entirety. There were several aluminums sinks and cold, lifeless bodies lying underneath white sheets with tags on their big toes. Being around so many dead people didn't have any effect on Fear. It was something that he was used to given his lifestyle. He knew with the life he led that one day he'd eventually find himself lying here among these poor souls.

Fear and Italia followed the autopsy technician who led them to a metal table at the end of a row of corpses. autopsy technician was a short, big headed balding man totting a clipboard and popping bubble gum. The autopsy technician looked at his clipboard and then at the tag hanging around the toe of the corpse at the last table. Seeing that the identification tag matched, he walked over to the head of the table and drew the sheet back. His removal of the sheet revealed Master Hahn who was hideously burned, almost to no recognition.

"Is this him?" the autopsy technician asked Fear.

"Yeah, it's him. Good old Master Hahn," Fear said regretfully, tears pouring down his face.

"I'm so sorry, baby." Italia told him, hugging him affectionately.

Fear didn't say a word. He just stood there continuing to cry. The pain he felt was kin to how he felt when his father died from cancer. All he ever knew was pain and death. And given his current occupation he knew he'd better get used to it because times weren't going to change for as long as he played the game he was in.

Italia whipped out a silk pink handkerchief and dabbed away the tears from her fiancé's eyes. She then kissed him on the cheek.

He turned to her and kissed her back before walking over to Master Hahn's body. He kissed the old man on his forehead.

I'ma find the mothafucka that got at chu and I'ma make 'em pay for this. I swear if it's the last thing I do, vengeance will be mine. I put that on my honor. Rest easy. I love you, OG.

Fear kissed him on his forehead again. The autopsy technician covered Master Hahn's body back up with the sheet. He then handed the clipboard over to Fear and he signed some paperwork. Afterwards, Fear and Italia were led out of the morgue.

Later, Fear would have Master Hahn's body cremated and

placed inside of a solid gold urn which he had his name branded on in Japanese letters. He placed the urn on top of the mantle above his fireplace, inside of his home.

CHAPTER FIVE

The next night

Big Sexy made his way out of the house to head to Subway to get himself a sandwich. He locked the door to his house and hustled down the steps whistling, still holding his keys in his hand. He made his way around the corner of his house, to get his car in the driveway and ran into two dark figures about ten feet away from him. He couldn't tell who the people were. But he could tell that both were holding baseball bats. Both of which Big Sexy had no intentions of going up against, if he had any say so in the matter.

Big Sexy's survival instincts kicked in and he pulled his handgun from out of his waistline. He went to point it at the dark figures as they moved in on him, but someone crept up behind him with a baseball bat, ready to swing.

Thwop!

"Uhhhh!" Big Sexy belted out and winced, feeling the wooden bat strike him across the back of the skull. He dropped his handgun to the ground and crashed to the pavement. Slowly, he tried to get back up but the mothafucka that had cracked him in the back of the head, stood over him, bringing the bat down again and again. It wasn't long after the dark figures who were at the other end of the driveway joined in, beating him with their baseball bats.

While this was going on, in the background, there was Gunplay. He was wearing a blue bandana around his forehead and a hood over his head. He stuck a cigarette inside of his mouth and cupped his hand around it as he lit it up. He took a pull from off the square and caused the tip of it to turn ember. His cheeks puffed up with smoke which he blew out into the air. He watched attentively as Big Sexy got the dog shit beat out of him. Once Gunplay figured he'd taken enough of a beating, he dropped his

Joe at his sneaker and mashed it out.

"Alright, that's enough! Pull 'em up on his knees." Gunplay said as he walked towards Big Sexy, pulling out his handgun and cocking that shit. When the thugs held Big Sexy up on his knees, his face and head were twice the size they naturally were. The big man was bloody about the face and two strings of bloody, slimy saliva hung from his chin to his shirt. His left eye was swollen shut so he only had his slightly opened right eye to see through. The pupil in it moved around aimlessly as he moaned in pain.

Gunplay grabbed Big Sexy by the lower half of his face causing his lips to pucker up like he wanted a kiss. The young gangsta then forced his gun inside of his mouth and stared him in the eyes, mad dogging him. "Look at me, look at me, you snitch ass mothafucka!" Big Sexy's good eye focused on Gunplay, going in and out of focus. The big man was on the brink of passing out, but there was something deep within him that was keeping him alert. "If it wasn't for the fact that popping you right now would break my nigga Fear's heart, I'd do yo right now and leave you for roaches and rats to feast off of, you hear me?"

Big Sexy didn't say shit and he was rewarded by Gunplay smacking him with the side of his handgun, knocking him out cold. While the big man lay on the ground in a heap, Gunplay and all his thugs harped up phlegm and spat on his face. The warm nasty goo splattered on Big Sexy's face as he lay there unconscious. As Gunplay and his thugs walked away police car sirens filled the air. The police were late like they always were when something went down in the ghetto, and Gunplay and his thugs were gone.

***

Italia was behind the wheel of Fear's car while he played the passenger seat, scanning the parking lot of the Food 4 Less on Normandie and Western, waiting for Gunplay to arrive. Being blinded by the bright orbs of an oncoming car, pulling inside of the parking lot, Fear narrowed his eyelids. He then placed his hand above his eyebrows so he could get a good look at who was approaching him. Seeing that it was Gunplay's car, he hopped out of his whip and slammed the door shut behind him.

Gunplay swung his car recklessly beside Fear's car, like he was in a hurry, making his tires screech to a halt. Hastily, the young nigga hopped out of the car and bopped his way over to Fear, Big Sexy's paperwork in hand. Fear could tell by the look on his face that he meant business, so he wondered what was on his mind. Gunplay shoved the paperwork into Fear's chest which made him frown up. Fear took the papers and started looking over them, the more he read, the further he frowned.

"Where you get this from?" Fear asked Gunplay, and he told him. "How do you know it's real?"

Gunplay's face balled up and he paced the ground, running his hands down his face, frustrated. He stopped before Fear and said, "You see, I knew you were gonna act like this once I brought this snitch ass nigga to yo attention. It's hard for you to believe it 'cause he's yo right-hand man!"

Fear looked through the paperwork again, reading every sheet of it. The more he read, the more he hurt, and the more he hurt the more he wanted to kill Big Sexy's ass for being a rat. Out of all the people in the world the snitch had to be him. He hated him for that fact. He hated him because he knew it wasn't going to be so easy for him to pull the trigger on him. You see, had it been anyone else, including Gunplay, he'd have no trouble splitting their wig. But that wasn't the case. The traitor was a man he'd loved like he came from the same womb as him.

Fear folded up the paperwork and stuck it into his back pocket, saying, "I'ma take care of this."

"What chu mean you gon' take care of it? Exactly what the fuck are you gonna do?" Gunplay inquired.

"Since when in the fuck did, I start answering to you? You better check yo self, lil' nigga. Now, I said I'ma handle this shit, let's leave it at that." Fear mad dogged him for a while before jumping back into the passenger seat and slamming the door shut behind him. He gave Italia the signal to pull off, but Gunplay jogged over to the car and stopped them. He told Fear about letting his thugs beat the brakes off Big Sexy and leaving him for dead. "So, where is he at now?" Fear asked him.

"I don't know. If I had to guess I would say a hospital." Gunplay told him.

"Alright, man." Fear motioned for Italia to drive off and she followed his orders. While she was whipping through the streets, he told her what was on the paperwork. She shook her head pitifully. She also couldn't believe that Big Sexy ratted. Out of all the niggaz Fear had under him, she believed that Big Sexy was the most loyal and trustworthy, but unfortunately, he'd proven her wrong.

Fear pulled out his cellular and started hitting up hospitals in Los Angeles County. "I'll tell you; these days you can't trust anyone."

Italia looked at him. Grasping his hand, she looked at him with a serious expression and said, "You can trust me."

"I know, baby." He kissed her. Right after, he heard someone pick up the telephone at Centinela Hospital. He gave them Big Sexy's government name and they told him they didn't have anyone there by that name. Fear went on to hit up a dozen or so hospitals until he found out where his right-hand man was. Once he'd gotten off the cell phone, he told Italia to swing him by his house so he could get something. Italia obliged him without further questioning him.

***

Fear walked inside Big Sexy's room, switching hands with the Nike duffle bag and shutting the door behind him. His best friend, Big Sexy, looked at him and dapped him up, thanking him for coming out to see him.

"Not that I'm not happy to see you, but how'd you know I was here?" Big Sexy's forehead creased with curiosity, and he sat up in bed. He was wearing a powder blue hospital gown and had a hospital issued information band around his right wrist. From the swelling and bruising on his face, you could tell he'd taken one hell of a beating from Gunplay and his thug ass homeboys.

"I called around until I was given your location." Fear told him as he pulled up a chair and sat down beside his bed.

"I gotchu. But how did you know I was here in the first place?"

Fear gave Big Sexy a look like *Come on now, my nigga, obviously I know you're snitching.*

"I've already seen the paperwork, but I'd like to hear it from the horse's mouth."

Big Sexy frowned up and said, "What're you talking about?"

Fear shot him a look that let him know that he already knew what he was getting at, but the nigga still fronted on him. So, he reached inside of his back pocket and pulled out the paperwork with his name all over it, dropping it down on Big Sexy's chest. Big Sexy picked the paperwork up and his heart sunk to his stomach. He swallowed the lump of nervousness in his throat and tears instantly filled his eyes. He then looked to Fear, wetness sliding down his cheeks. "All I can say is that mothafucka had me by the balls, man. I was fucked, and there wasn't any way that I could get outta it."

"Besides, ratting on me, right?" Fear jumped to his feet and pulled a Glock from the small of his back, placing it to the center of Big Sexy's forehead. "Act like you hear me when I'm talking to you, nigga. Speak!"

"Yes! Yes, yes, I gave you up to save my own ass, and I'm sorry, bro. I'm so, so fucking sorry!"

Fear stared down at Big Sexy, mad dogging him as tears escaped down his cheeks and dripped onto the floor, splashing. His eyes were pink and red web from his blood pressure being so high. He had a lot on his shoulders. Knowing that his best friend turned state on him fucked him up that much more. All he could think about was how he had sold him out. After all they'd been through together, he had it in him to sail him up the fucking river. Life was a bitch. Nah, life was a cold-hearted bitch named Debra, with great, big titties and an even bigger ass. "I should blow yo fucking brains out of the back of yo fucking head, you rat bastard! You were supposed to have been my dawg! My mothafucking brother from another, but chu turned out to be a diseased ridden, sniveling fucking weasel." He shook his head and wiped away the tears that dripped from the brims of his eyes. He then sniffled, slowly pulling back on the trigger.

Seeing Fear's finger pulling back on the trigger, Big Sexy grabbed him by the hand he held the gun with, startling him. Big Sexy pressed the deadly end of the gun into his forehead and squeezed his eyelids shut as tears slid down his cheeks, and green snot threatened to drip from out of his nostrils. "Go ahead and do yo thang, man. I deserve it, for the shit I did. Gon' and do it, bro! Puff my mothafucking wig out." He squeezed his eyelids tighter and bit down on his bottom lip, waiting for the shot to be fired that would end his life for all eternity. The next thing he knew, Fear was flipping the gun around in his hand and outstretching it toward him. A surprised look came over Big Sexy face, wondering if it was some kind of trick. He looked back and forth between the handgun and the sorrowful expression on Fear's face. "Go ahead and take it." He brought the gun further to Big Sexy and he snatched it. The big man watched Fear closely as he picked up the Nike duffle bag, he'd brought into the room with him and sat it down on Big Sexy's chest. He unzipped the bag and held it open for Big Sexy to look inside of it, which he did. "That's one hundred grand, right there. I want chu to take it and get the fuck outta L.A. You can't stay here anymore, everybody and their baby's momma is looking to take yo head for ratting me out. Once you get outta dodge, never look back, stay gone. Don't chu ever dare to show your face around here again. Do you understand me?"

"Yeah, I understand," Big Sexy said, pulling the bag into him and stashing his Glock inside of it.

Fear clutched either side of Big Sexy's head and stared deep into his eyes, saying, "Nah, nigga, I don't think you hear me. I need to hear you say it. I need you to say, yes, Al, I fucking understand you. I'm gonna get my shit and get the fuck outta dodge. You'll never have to see my ugly fucking face again. So go on. Go on and tell me, right fucking now."

"Yes, Al, I fucking understand," Big Sexy began. "I'm gonna get my shit and get the fuck outta dodge. You'll never have to see my fucking face again."

"Good." Fear hugged him and more tears slid down his face. He held his embrace for what seemed like an eternity, before kissing him on his forehead. He pulled away from him and straightened out the wrinkles in his hospital gown. "I love you, my nigga."

"I love you, too." Big Sexy spoke from the heart. He then looked over Fear's shoulder expecting a hitter to enter the room and blow his brains out. You couldn't have told him that his best friend wasn't setting him up to be murdered after finding out he'd squealed on him.

Fear's glassy, pink eyes lingered on Big Sexy for a minute longer before he walked out of the room.

Big Sexy knew that by him being a snitch that his reputation in the street was ruined. There wasn't anything that he could do about that. But he could right a few wrongs and leave an impact on the streets before his departure. Right there in that hospital bed, he vowed to himself to make the streets feel him…one last time.

The next day

Gustavo sat on his living room couch in his robe, legs crossed. He indulged in a Cuban cigar. Taking the occasional pull from the overgrown cancer stick, he blew out a cloud of smoke and continued to watch television. Well, he wasn't really watching television. It was more like it was watching him. You see, Gustavo was a thinking man. And right now, he was thinking about what had occurred the other night between him and Esteban. He didn't have anything to do with that mothafucka's shipment getting hit, all those times. In fact, each time it happened he doubled up on security on the load, but that still didn't stop poachers from taking it.

As of right now, Gustavo was trying to figure out who it was that hit Esteban's shipment of cocaine. And how did they know where the drop was being made? Once he figured that out, he was sure that the traitor would reveal himself. And once they did, there would be hell to pay for their betrayal. Just thinking about a mothafucka playing him like a fucking fiddle angered Gustavo. His eyebrows slanted and his nose crinkled as he gritted his teeth, holding the cigar wedged between his fingers, smoke wafting around him.

Knock, knock, knock, knock!

Rapping at the door caused Gustavo to snap back to reality. When he looked down, he saw embers from his cigar burning through the leg of his silk pajamas. He yelped and hopped to his feet, smacking the embers from off his leg. "God damn it!"

Knock, knock, knock, knock!

"Hold on, gemme a sec." Gustavo dabbed out his cigar in the ashtray and made his way towards the front door. He peered through the peephole and saw the mail man. He relaxed a little seeing who it was because he was still uptight since the beef kicked off with Esteban. Although Esteban was a small fry compared to him and the niggaz he'd bumped heads with over the years, he didn't make any illusions to what a man could do in the heat of battle when he was desperate to win.

What the fuck am I so edgy about? I've got shooters up the asshole; they wouldn't let any of my enemies get through those gates. AKs, AR-15s, M-4s; shiiiiit, they'd eat those bastards alive, Gustavo thought as he unchained and unlocked the door. Once he pulled the thick door open, he found the mail man holding a big box for him, with a clipboard on top of it.

"Good afternoon." The mail man greeted him smiling.

"Good afternoon." Gustavo replied.

"I've gotta package for you. I just need you to sign this form and she's all yours." He showed him the form which was clamped to the clipboard. Gustavo took the clipboard and signed his signature on it. Afterwards, he gave the mail man a few dollars as a tip and took the box from him, kicking the front door shut. He then journeyed inside of the kitchen where he sat the box down on the counter. Grabbing a butcher's knife from out of the knife block, he sliced the box opened down the middle and broke the Scotch tape that held it sealed closed. He sat the butcher's knife aside and dipped his hands inside of the box which was filled to the brim with Styrofoam chips. His brow creased as he fished around inside of the box for what was inside. Gripping whatever had been delivered to him with both hands, Gustavo pulled out what was clutched in his hands and spilled Styrofoam chips back inside of the box.

Gustavo was shocked to see that he was holding one of his goons' severed heads in his hands. It was the same goon whose kneecaps were shot out by Esteban's goon. The eyes of the goon's were rolled to the left and his tongue was hanging out of his mouth in a grotesque manner. Gustavo dropped the severed head back into the box it came in. He then ran back up to the front door and opened it, looking around for the mail man that had delivered the package. That mothafucka was long gone though.

Gustavo looked at the other end of his porch at the goon that was there and whistled, "Yo!" waving for him to come forward. Once the goon came forward, he told him to stand right at the door while he disappeared inside of the mansion. He came back with the box that contained the goon's severed head and gave it to the goon that was posted up outside of the door.

"Discard it." Gustavo looked around his estate as he brushed imaginary dust from off his hands before ducking back inside of the mansion, slamming and locking the door behind him.

***

"Look, I'ma cut to the chase, I'm not gonna beat around the bush," Gustavo began. "I know you've been training to kill, and I need some people dead. Now, seeing that you're new to the

contract killing business, I figure that I could put you in touch with some business acquaintances of mine that will keep your waist deep in work. But that's only if you handle this floating piece of shit that I have in mind." he said as he clipped the tip of his cigar off and lit it up with a custom 14k gold Zippo lighter. He blew out a cloud of smoke and sat the lighter down on the desktop.

"If doing business with you is going to put me in line to do more business than I'm all ears, jefe," Fear assured Gustavo as he called him 'boss' in Spanish.

"Good. Now that's what I like to hear."

"So, who is the piece of shit you need me to get off your lawn?"

"Esteban Gomez. I need you to take care of him and his entire family for me." Gustavo dabbed out his cigar inside of the ashtray and pulled out a photograph of Esteban, his wife and kid, handing it to Fear. Fear stood in front of the desk looking over the photograph. Out of all his time in the streets he'd never killed a kid before. And he wasn't going to start to now. He'd go along with what Gustavo wanted if he could get him a list of contacts of people who were interested in hiring him as a gun. Sure, he still had the cell phone that Hahn had given him. But the people Gustavo knew were playing at a different level. They were some major players so he was sure he could charge them a nice bag for anyone whose head they wanted knocked off their shoulders. Sure enough, Gustavo didn't say this, but Fear believed that a gangsta of his caliber was sure to have some pretty strong ties to some very important people. That was for damn sure. "Is this going to be a problem for you?" Gustavo leaned back in his big black leather executive officer chair smoking his cigar and blowing smoke rings.

"No. Not at all. I have a question though."

"Shoot."

"With all of the goons you have on yo payroll, why didn't you just have one of them take out your trash?"

"Should they get caught, it will put the police right on my trail."

Fear nodded and said, "Smart man."

"It took a lot of favors, but I was able to obtain his address. It's on the back of the photograph." Gustavo pointed to the photograph. Fear picked up the photograph and flipped it over, memorizing the address. He handed the photograph back to

Gustavo and he frowned up. "Don't chu want this so you'll know what they look like? You'd at least need the address."

Fear tapped his temple and grinned, saying, "It's all up here, my man. I don't wanna get caught with that. That's some very incriminating evidence."

"Riiiiight," Gustavo nodded. "So, what do I owe you for this…business transaction?"

"Since homie is sort of a big deal, gemme a two-hunnit bands."

"Done."

"Half up front, the other half once the gig is done."

"Sounds good to me, lemme get that for you."

Gustavo left and returned with a small duffle bag filled with money. Fear didn't even bother to count the loot. He slapped hands with Gustavo and went on about his business. Getting back inside of his whip, he sat the duffle bag into Italia's lap and she looked through the bag while he pushed the wheel.

"How much is this?" Italia asked as she thumbed through a

stack of dead faces.

"That's a hunnit large." Fear told her. He then went on to tell her what he had to do for it. He wanted to see the look on her face when he told her he had to murder a kid, surprisingly Italia didn't flinch. She seemed to be cool with the idea. And that was something that didn't quite sit well with Fear. He reasoned that she was down for him and everything else paled when compared to their love for one another. When he thought of it that way then it made perfectly good sense to him.

"If you going after more than one person then I'ma roll witchu, you're definitely going to need some back up." She told him, making perfectly good sense. "And don't tell me no 'cause I'm not taking no for an answer. I'm rolling witchu and that's final."

"Okay." Fear relented.

"Okay?" She looked at him surprised. She was expecting to get a fight out of him, but to her surprise he was okay with her rolling with him.

"Now gemme a kiss." They pecked on the lips.

Fear continued to drive while Italia counted the money they'd

gotten for the hit.

That night

The lights were out inside Broli's bedroom as he lay in bed, eating a bowl of chocolate chip ice cream. The light illuminating from the "50-inch flat screen danced across the upper half of him as he watched the Entourage movie. Having finished his ice cream, he hopped out of bed and slipped his corduroy house shoes on, making his way down his dimly lit hallway. Walking inside of the kitchen, he flipped on the light switch and sat the bowl down inside of the sink. He grabbed a glass from out of the cupboard, filled it with ice, and took his bottle of Hennessy down.

Broli filled his glass halfway with Hennessy and took a sip. As soon as he brought the glass to his lips, a gloved hand smacked it out of his hand. The glass exploded against the wall, sending broken glass and alcohol flying everywhere. When Broli turned back around a masked man whacked him behind his right knee with a cattle prod, causing him to bend backwards. The masked man followed up by whacking him across the back of the head. Broli hit the floor on his face wincing, out cold.

The masked man tucked the cattle prod inside of his belt and dragged an unconscious Broli back inside of his bedroom. Using four different leather belts, he then tied Broli's wrists and ankles to the bedposts. Afterwards, the masked man splashed him in the face with a big ass bucket of water. As soon as the cold water hit Broli's face, his head shot up from off the mattress. The crooked detective looked around batting his eyelashes and gasping for air. He shook the water loose from his face and looked ahead where he saw a masked man. His vision came into focus, and he saw the man clearly. He was dressed in all black and holding a cattle prod at his side. From the way the nigga was staring at him through the holes in his mask, he knew that he meant business and he was about to wish he was never born. Especially when he realized he was not only tied up to the bed posts, but he was butt ass naked, dick hanging out.

"Bruh, do you know who you playin' with? Huh? Do you? Nigga, I'm One Time!" Broli looked at him like *You are making a big mistake.*

"Yeah, I know. And I must say that I don't give a fuck." The masked man tossed Broli's badge onto his chest and pulled off his ski mask, revealing his identity. It was Big Sexy.

"Big man? That's you?" Broli's forehead wrinkled as he looked at Big Sexy. He couldn't believe that the big man had the balls to pull the stunt he was pulling.

"Yeah, it's me, you cocksucka! And you gon' tell me what I wanna know, or I'm gonna make you as useless as an asshole on an elbow below the waist." Big Sexy said, referring to him making it so that Broli could never satisfy a woman sexually.

"Nigga, I swear on Jesus' sandals, if you do anything to me I'ma make it my life's duty to fuck yo life…ahhhhhhhh!"

Big Sexy zapped Broli's nut sack with the cattle prod causing him to scream at the top of his lung, little thing at the back of his throat shaking uncontrollably. Every cavity inside of Broli's mouth could be seen from him opening his mouth so wide and screaming so goddamn loud.

"Shut cho bitch ass up and listen to what the fuck I gotta say." Big Sexy told him. "Now, look, I know you got that file on Alvin Simpson so I'ma need you to delete that shit. As well as burn whatever copies you have left."

"Okay, okay, but first I'ma need you to—I'ma need you to—"

Broli huffed and puffed out of breath as his chest expanded and shrunk for each breath that he took.

"You're gonna need me to what?" Big Sexy asked, looking serious as fuck.

"I'ma gonna need you to suck my dick, you bitch ass nigga!" he snarled hatefully.

"Always the theatrics witchu," Big Sexy rolled his eyes annoyed and zapped Broli's nut sack again. In fact, he zapped his sack again, again and again, until his crooked ass agreed to do what he told him to.

Broli hacked into the police system's database, like he'd been doing for years with his crooked black ass. He brought up the file he had on Alvin 'Fearless' Simpson and deleted it before Big Sexy's eyes. Afterwards, he dumped every last file he had inside of the house on Fear inside of the fireplace along with the burning logs. Once he done this, Big Sexy motioned for him to sit down with a handgun he'd just pulled from his waistline. He obliged.

Once Broli had sat down on the couch, Big Sexy pulled his cell phone from out of his pocket and set it to record. He then sat down on the opposite couch, staring directly into Broli's fearless eyes.

"I want chu to tell me the addresses of every crooked badge that was helping you hit those shipments of cocaine you were pawning off on me to sell." Big Sexy told him. As soon as the command was given, Broli went on to give him the names and addresses of the shady cops that were helping him steal shipments of cocaine. "Good looking out, my nigga."

"You gonna leave now?" Broli asked him.

"Yep."

Boc!

A bullet ripped through Broli's gut causing him to make an ugly ass face and double over. He bled at the mouth and held his side, looking up at Big Sexy accusingly, wincing.

"You dirty mothafucka, you know what they give nigga that kill law enforcement officers, huh?"

"Yeah. The needle!" Big Sexy shot up to his feet and extended his handgun, pulling the trigger. He put two holes into Broli's forehead and left the house through the way he'd gotten in—the window.

CHAPTER SIX

Gunplay came through the door of his apartment switching hands with his small brown paper bag of items. He shut the door behind him and locked it, walking over to the kitchen table, which was sitting just outside of the kitchen, in the living room. Gunplay sat his brown paper bag down on the kitchen table and flipped on the light switch. The light from the kitchen partially illuminated the kitchen table, leaving the rest of the living room in darkness.

Gunplay turned on the small radio sitting on the kitchen counter, flipping through the channels until he found Lloyd Banks' *Can I get high.* Having found something he was comfortable to listen to while rolling up that sticky icky, he sat down at the kitchen table and emptied the contents out from the small brown paper bag. Inside of the bag there was an ounce of weed, two Swisher Sweets, a 5th of Hennessy and a couple of plastic cups.

Gunplay opened his ounce of weed and dipped his head low, inhaling the intoxicating scent coming from out of it. He closed his eyelids briefly and a smile spread across his face, enchanted by the pretty green buds' aroma. Sitting the ounce back down on the tabletop, he went to break some of the weed down, but remembered that he didn't have anything to break the shit down on. Snapping his fingers, Gunplay rose from the chair and headed into the living room to get the XXL magazine from off the coffee table. He'd gotten halfway there when a red laser extended across the room, producing a red dot on his forehead.

Gunplay froze up as soon as he saw the red laser coming from the dark figure sitting on his living room couch. He was stunned. He slowly placed his hands up into the air, eyes wide and mouth open, hoping he didn't get his brain blown out.

Suddenly, the dark figure leaned over the arm of the couch and clicked on the lamp light. Once the light came on, it was revealed that it was Big Sexy behind the trigger of the infrared laser beam. He wore the hood of his Nike hoodie enclosed around his head and his face was masked by seriousness.

"I thought you woulda been on yo shit, youngsta. But a nigga caught chu with your pants down." Big Sexy told him. "You holding?"

"Nah, fam, I left my shit in the car, under the driver's seat. See for yourself." Gunplay told him.

"No need for all of that, G. I believe you."

There was silence between the two of them and it was practically driving Gunplay insane.

"So, what's up, cuz? You gon' handle yo business or what?" he inquired of the big man shooting him.

"Nah, man, I'm leaving the game and I just wanted to leave you a parting gift."

"Why the fuck would you gemme a gift after I done told everybody and their momma that chu a mothafucking snitch?"

"I hear you," Big Sexy told him. "I did some thinking and I can't even be mad witchu about that. You did what you were supposed to do. You warned the family about a traitor they had in the midst. I can respect that. And had the shoe been on the other foot, I woulda done the same."

Gunplay looked at him like he was crazy, forehead creasing with lines.

Cuz, this shit has got to be a trick. Aint no way this nigga gon' let me walk without putting one in my head. No way. Get the fuck outta here, Gunplay thought to himself as he continued to hold his hands in the air, keeping his eyes on Big Sexy.

Gunplay was startled when he saw Big Sexy reach inside of his pocket. He started to make a run for it, but the big man put him at ease by telling him to relax. He then came out of his pocket with a key that had a storage number key ring on it. He dangled it before Gunplay's eyes and said, "See, it's just a key." He tossed the key over to Gunplay and he caught it. He then opened his palm and looked down at the key. The storage unit was F-146 and it was located at Dynasty Self Storage.

"What's this to? I mean, what's inside of the storage unit?" A curious Gunplay asked him.

"Your future," Big Sexy turned the red dot off Gunplay's forehead and rose from the couch. Walking past him, Big Sexy patted him on his shoulder and continued towards the front door, tucking his banga inside of his waistline.

The next day

The Starbucks on Crenshaw and Rosecrans was scarce with patrons mainly because the establishment was a known hangout spot for notoriously crooked cops. You could catch the likes of narcotics detectives Spellman, Brady, Kingsly, Creedy here on and off duty enjoying their favorite ice-cold beverage and shooting the shit like a couple of old college buddies. Now, they were all sitting at the table taking casual sips of their beverages while the eldest of them, Creedy, told them about how he had some college babe bent over the hood of his car, giving her the old hard-one.

"I'm tellin' you, man, this broad was blowtorch hot," Creedy made faces to illustrate exactly how attractive the young blonde, big breasted chick was he'd taken out the night before. "I pulled out my cock and shot my load right on her double D's and her face, and I was still raging bull hard. Good to go another round. I'll tell ya, fellas, young pussy is an older man's aphrodisiac and fountain of youth." He picked up his Caramel Macchiato and took a sip from his straw.

The bell sounded as a hooded man walked inside of the establishment. Instantly, Detective Creedy's eyes were on him because he was African American and looked 'suspicious'. The man stepped on line behind the rest of the patrons. Detective Creedy nudged Brady and nodded to the hooded man. This created a domino effect, which all the crooked detectives turned their eyes on the man.

"Aye, buddy, do me a favor and take that hood off of your head!" Creedy called out from where he was sitting and drew all the patrons' attention. He was hoping that the hooded man would defy him so he could rough him up and haul his ass down to the station. His conversation with his boys was getting stale and he was looking for some action.

The hooded man acted like he didn't hear Creedy and continued to stand online unbothered.

"Aye buddy, why don't chu do me a favor and take off your hood!" Creedy called out again, sitting up in his chair. He was getting upset now. He was used to people doing what he said once he had said it once. He wasn't used to repeating himself. His ego was getting the best of him now. He was in fear of the man in the hood making him look bad in front of his peers.

The other detectives at the table chuckled and laughed. Detective Brady turned to Creedy and said, "Hey, Creedy, I think that's his way of telling you to go fuck yourself!" The table erupted in great laughter then. Right after, a very pissed off Creedy scooted away from the table and shot to his feet, making his way towards the hooded man with his hand on his holstered gun. He got five feet away from him before he unbuckled the strap from his handgun.

"Look, asshole, I know you heard me when I told you to—gaaggg" Creedy was cut short as his eyes bulged and his mouth dropped open. The hooded man, which was really, Big Sexy, karate chopped him in the throat. Instantly, Creedy grabbed his neck with both hands. Big Sexy followed up by kicking him in his crotch. He howled in pain, grabbing himself and dropping to his knees. Swiftly, Big Sexy grabbed his handgun from where it was holstered on his hip. He pulled Creedy into him, turned him around and placed his gun at the top of his head. Creedy stood on his knees, facing the other detectives, tears rolling, still holding himself.

"Ah, ah, ah, mothafuckaz!" Big Sexy called out to the detectives, seeing them about to draw heat. "Y'all up them guns, nice and easy, and slide them shits this way." While the detectives did what Big Sexy demanded, the patrons and the employees stood around looking petrified of what was to come. Once he'd gotten all the detectives' guns by him, Big Sexy said to the patrons and employees. "Everyone else, I want chu to get the fuck up outta here, this doesn't concern you so don't try to be a hero! Now, gone and get outta here!"

The patrons and the employees cleared the Starbucks, leaving Big Sexy and the crooked ass detectives in the establishment.

Blowl, blowl, blowl!

Big Sexy's eyes got as big as saucers having taken three in his back. His mouth hung open and he dropped his handgun. He released Creedy and fell to the floor, bleeding out of his mouth. Standing behind him was rookie detective Stephens. All the coffee he'd drunk had gotten the best of his bladder and he'd excused himself to take a piss just before Big Sexy had arrived. This is how he'd gotten the drop on the big man.

The rest of the detectives rushed over and picked up their guns. They all helped a red faced and wheezing Creedy to his feet, handing him his handgun back.

"Are you okay, sir?" Stephens asked him, holstering his handgun.

"Yeah. Are you all right?" Kingsly asked, looking concerned.

Creedy nodded as he continued to massage his neck. "I'll be—I'll be fine."

"No thanks to this piece of shit!" Brady kicked Big Sexy in his side. He then switched hands with his gun and pulled Big Sexy over onto his back. He found himself staring down at Big Sexy who was smiling devilishly, four metal rings in his mouth. Brady's eyes got big when he noticed that Big Sexy was holding two pineapple grenades in either of his hands.

"Oh, n—" Brady was cut short as the grenades exploded. Fire rushed out of every window and door of Starbucks and entered the streets.

Rest In Peace Big Sexy!

That night

Gunplay drove up inside Dynasty Self Storage and checked in with the clerk, signing in. He then jogged back outside to his car and hopped in, slamming the door shut behind him. He coasted by rows and rows of shutters to storage units on either side of him. His neck was on a swivel, scanning both sides for the storage unit number he was looking for: F-146. He repeated the number to himself over and over again, until he finally reached it. The storage unit was on his right. He kept his whip running as he hopped out of it, making his way around the car and then unlocking the lock that held the shutter shut. Once he pulled the shutter open, he stepped inside and closed it. He pulled out his cellular and used its flashlight to see inside of the storage, shining its light on everything inside. There was a sofa, a reclining chair, a piano and bench, and four large boxes. Gunplay used a small pocketknife to open the first box, which had a beach towel lying over the top of it. When he removed the towel, his eyes grew as big as dinner plates and his mouth hung open. He dipped his hand inside of the box and came back up with a brick of cocaine wrapped in cellophane. A grin spread across his lips.

Gunplay dropped the brick back down inside of the box and went through the others. They were all filled with bricks of cocaine. He held the first brick of the last box up like it was gold, admiring it.

"Yeahhhhh, boy, it's about to be on now. Nigga, 'bout to make it snow in Cali." Gunplay smiled hard. All his life he'd been the young gunner holding it down for The Man in his neighborhood.

Now he was about to be *The Man.*

My, my, my how the tables have turned!

***

Fear and Italia had themselves a drink and put some Loud in the air. Right after, they got ready for the assignment that Gustavo had hired Fear for. They strapped on bulletproof vests and got dressed in all black fatigues. They then loaded and locked their MP-5's, holstered .45 automatics and stashed extra magazines on them. Next, they headed out of the house and climbed into Fear's whip, driving off the block. They weren't worried about anybody spotting them dressed how they were because they were behind limo tinted window glass.

Fear made a left turn on 42nd and Halldale Avenue. Cruising down the block, he looked from left to right as he tried to find a Gride for the night's mission. Finding one he was satisfied with, a smile spread across his face. The vehicle he had in mind, a black Yukon Denali, reflected on the driver's window. Fear parked his car across the street and down the block from the car he had in mind to steal. Grabbing what he'd need to pop the locks on that mothafucka, he and his lady hopped out of his whip and slammed the doors shut. Hunching over, they hastily made their way across the street, looking around for anyone that may be watching them break the law. Once they didn't see anyone, they continued towards the vehicle. Fear stopped at the driver's door while Italia went around to the front passenger door. Using his tool, Fear popped the locks on the Yukon Denali and hotwired it. The vehicle roared to life and NWA's *Chin Check* thumped from its speakers. After throwing the car into *drive*, he looked into the side view mirror to see if any vehicles were coming. Once he didn't see anyone, he pulled out of the parking space and drove off.

An hour and a half later Fear ended up at a gated community where there was an on-duty security guard. He passed him a wrinkled brown paper back out of the driver's window and the security guard opened it, seeing stacks and stacks of dead white men inside. He nodded his satisfaction to Fear and pressed the button that made the black iron gate slide back. He then killed the surveillance cameras that were on sight monitoring everything. "You've got fifteen minutes." The bald-headed security guard told him in a hushed tone. Fear nodded and continued in over the threshold of the gated community, killing his headlights. He parked on the other side of the house that he and his lady had to hit, bodying the engine. Italia popped open the glove box and grabbed two ski masks, handing her nigga one. They pulled them shits over their heads and straightened the eye holes on them so that they could see out of them correctly. Next, Fear popped the trunk, and they hopped out, making their way to its rear. They opened the trunk and took out two MP-5s. They made sure them hoes were loaded, cocked and locked before Fear slammed the trunk shut.

"Come here," Fear pulled Italia close to him, kissing her deep, hard and passionately. "I love yo fine ass."

"I love you more, boo. Enough of that lovey dovey shit. Let's go handle our business." Italia told him.

"A gangsta bitch. I love it." He smacked her on the ass, and they hunched down, making their way towards Esteban's house. They crossed the front yard, and the backyard of the house on the other sides of Esteban's house. They saw a couple of people talking and swigging beers while one of them flipped whatever meat was on the grill. Thankfully it was dark outside, and the bushes were camouflaging Fear and Italia. Otherwise, they would have been seen, but that wasn't the case. Fear and Italia scaled the separating gate and landed on the other side of it on their bending knees. Hunched down, they moved in on everyone in the backyard, taking them out with muffled gunshots. Once everyone in the backyard had been executed, they met up at the backdoor, hearing a host of people listening to what sounded like a boxing match on television. Italia stood upright on the side of the door, while Fear sat his weapon down and pulled out two pins. Keeping his eyes on the lock, he used the pins to pick it. The door popped open.

Once Fear had opened the back door, he put the pins up and opened the door. He and Italia eased inside of the kitchen, making their way towards the door just outside of the living room. They were about to enter the living room until a fat nigga rocking a cheap hair piece rose from the couch. He lumbered towards the kitchen swallowing the last of his Bud Light beer and burping. He came into the kitchen ignorant of Fear and Italia's presence, opening the refrigerator to get another beer. Fear passed Italia his MP-5, tip-toed across the kitchen floor and snatched a butcher's knife from out of the block on the counter. A gleam swept up the length of the big ass knife as he crept up on the fat man. The big nigga removed the cap off his beer with his teeth and spat it into the trashcan. As he brought the bottle to his lips, Fear pulled him back by his forehead and slit his meaty neck. The big man's eyes got as big as golf balls and his blood sprayed the white refrigerator.

Fear laid him down as gently as he could, but the short fall the fat bastard took caused his hair piece to fall halfway off his head.

Fear sat the butcher's knife beside his victim's body as his thick blood poured out of his neck like paint on the floor. Fear could see his reflection in the big man's blood as he crept back over to Italia and got his MP-5 from her. The couples stooped low where they were, listening to the people inside of the living room react to the fight. When Fear peeked his head around the corner and out of the doorway, he saw a woman and a little boy, who he gathered was Esteban's son, since he looked like him.

They were headed up the staircase. Fear figured the woman was Esteban's wife and she was taking the boy to pee upstairs.

"Okay," Fear turned to Italia, talking to her in a whisper. "A woman and a child went upstairs. I guess to use the bathroom from the way the boy was dancing around." "Alright," Italia nodded.

"There are five people in the living." Fear informed her. "Four of 'em are men. They're eating barbeque and drinking beer. Esteban is the nigga sitting in the recliner by himself, wearing a gold crown like he's a king or some shit. When we rush in, hit up everybody. Gustavo wants all of them niggaz dead. You Griff me?"

"I got chu."

"Okay. Move."

Fear and Italia swung out into the living room side by side, spitting heat. The mothafuckaz sitting inside of the living room never knew what hit them. All they heard were muffled guns shots and the sounds of hot metal hitting flesh. Blood, pieces of skulls and brain fragments splattered against the "60-inch flat screen which they were watching the boxing match on. Once the couple stopped firing, the living room was littered with dead bodies, blood and gun smoke. The only sound was the boxing match, which was still going on, bloody goop sliding down the television's screen.

"Mothafucka is still alive." Italia told Fear.

"Who?" Fear asked as he checked the other niggaz that they had shot up to see if they were truly dead. They were. When he turned around, he found Italia standing over Esteban. He was lying flat on his back bloody and looking grim about the face.

His chest rose up and down as he breathed, wheezing like he had asthma. "Stubborn one, aren't we?" Fear said of Esteban's refusal to die. "Watch 'em. I'll be right back."

Fear left the living room. He returned with a black garbage bag and the butcher's knife he'd used to cut the fat nigga's throat in the kitchen with. Fear busied himself cutting off Esteban's head so that he could deliver it to Gustavo the next time he met with him. Once he'd finished severing the kingpin's head and wrapping it up inside of the garbage bag, he looked over his shoulder to find that Italia had vanished.

"Ooooh, shiiit!"

***

Italia made her way up the staircase and onto the second level of the house. She went down the hallway cautiously, opening every bedroom and entering with her MP-5 ready to spit. Coming out of the last bedroom she'd entered; she came out and looked across the corridor again. Spotting a room she hadn't cleared yet, she decided to open it. As soon as Italia opened the hallway's closet door, a woman shoved her against the wall and ran down the corridor, pulling her son along with her. Italia looked down the hallway. She saw the woman fleeing with the little boy, running as fast as she could toward the staircase. Determined for her to not get away, Italia pointed her MP-5 at her back and squeezed the trigger. A spray of bullets splattered the woman's back and sent her falling awkwardly down the staircase with her son.

Italia ran down the hallway and down the staircase. On her way down, she saw the woman with tears in her eyes, squirming in pain. The little boy she was with winced and struggled to get to his feet, but he was hurt badly. Once Italia reached the landing, she pointed her MP-5 at the woman and finished her off. Having put her out of her misery, Italia turned her compact automatic weapon on the little boy. The youth couldn't be any older than four-years old, but Gustavo gave specific orders to murder Esteban's entire family.

"Noooooooooo!" Fear's voice ripped through the air. He dove across the living room and tackled Italia, before she could kill the child. Little mama's arm went up into the air and the MP-5 fired up at the ceiling, causing debris to trickle. Fear landed on top of Italia, breathing hard. "Fuck are you doing? He's just a kid. He's innocent!"

"Get the fuck off of me!" Italia shoved Fear off her and got to her feet. She looked him up and down like he was crazy. "Hell, you gon' come at me like that? I'm just following your orders. You said that Gustavo said to do his entire family, right? Well, this lil' boy is a descendant of his bloodline."

"That's right, baby, but I'm not killing no kids." Fear told her. "His blood won't stain either of our hands...you fine by that?" he asked Italia as he looked her square in her eyes. He kept eye contact with Italia, but his hand was slowly creeping towards his gun. If she tried to go through with murdering an innocent child, then he was going to leave her ass lying beside the boy's mother.

I love you to death, ma, but please don't put me in the position where I have to choose between you and this kid. Please.

"Yeah, I'm fine by that." Italia took a deep breath and ran her hand down her face. She then looked up at Fear, matching his gaze. "I'm sorry. You're right. He's just a kid. He's innocent. We can't kill 'em. But, babe, you know how crazy I am about chu. You said that Gustavo said that we're 'pose to knock off the whole fam. If we don't do it, then there could be hell to pay behind it. From what you told me he's a powerful man with many connections. That doesn't sound like someone you'd wanna run afoul of, you feel me?" she asked as she caressed the side of his

face lovingly.

"Lemme worry about that, baby. Okay?" "Okay." She nodded and they kissed.

Fear turned to the little boy and told him 'Night, night' before applying pressure to his temple and neck. These pressure points on the child's body caused him to fall right to sleep. The boy's eyelids shut, and he fell towards the floor. Before his small body could hit the surface, Fear scooped him up into his arms and carried him over to the couch. He laid the little dude down and looked at him for a while, eyes lingering on him. Standing there looking at the little boy, he imagined that the child was his son. And he couldn't imagine anyone bringing harm to his flesh and blood, because it would kill him mentally and physically.

"Come on. Let's get outta here." Fear motioned for Italia to follow him out of the house. She came along, and they fled into the night.

The next day

Fear pulled up alongside the curb on a residential street and hopped out of his car, making a beeline for one of Gustavo's goons, carrying Esteban's severed head in a brown paper shopping bag. The goon he was approaching was a tall ass nigga with a big bald head, which had tattoos on it. He was wearing big black sunglasses to shield his eyes from the beaming sun and a black Tshirt. He was posted up by himself, outside of a Mercedes-Benz van.

"What's up, Chico? Lemme get that other half of that paypa so I can slide up outta here, man." Fear told him, passing him the shopping bag.

"What's this?" his forehead wrinkled, holding the shopping bag open and peering inside of it.

"Confirmation of the kill," Fear told him as he scratched his temple. "Now, lemme get that so I can get up outta here." He looked around to make sure there weren't any cops around. There wasn't any police presence.

"I've got some bad news, big dawg."

"What chu mean you've got some bad news?" Fear's forehead creased.

"There isn't another bag, homie. You fucked up! You were supposed to have taken out the entire family. You left the kid alive." Chico looked at him like he was a stupid mothafucka.

"I couldn't kill an innocent child. That goes against my beliefs. Besides, I gave Gustavo the cat that he wanted. Esteban."

"Wrong answer!" Chico mad dogged him harder and pulled out an Uzi, pointing it at him. Fear lowered his head, looking up at the man with an evil expression on his face, holding up his hands in surrender. Right after, the sliding door of the van slid open and half of a dozen masked up dudes, in black fatigues, pointed AK-47s at Fear.

"Don't move, cocksucka!" One of the men shouted and snatched Fear's ass up, applying zip-cuffs to his wrists.

"What the fuck?" Italia's head popped up from where she was lying back in the seat, watching everything unfold.

Hurriedly, she popped open the glove box and grabbed her twin handguns, smacking the box shut. She hopped out of the car and aimed her guns at the niggaz' heads that were trying to kidnap her man.

Blowl, blowl!

The masked goons' heads and Chico's head snapped back upon impact of the bullets. They all collapsed to the ground and released Fear. Wrists still zip-cuffed behind his back, Fear tried to run away. He got five feet away before another goon jumped down from out of the van, AK-47 with a hundred round drum in hand. He kicked Fear in the back, and he fell to the asphalt. He then turned his AK-47 on Italia. He pulled the trigger of the deadly weapon, and it vibrated in his gloved hands. Italia dove to the ground as the AK-47 spitting lead shattered the parked car's windows and blew what looked like a billion holes in the side of it.

Italia sat up against the car with her head bowed, still gripping both guns. Her eyelids were squeezed shut and her jaws were locked. Fear's vehicle, which she was hiding behind, rocked back and forth from the fierce wave of bullets.

The goon relieved the trigger of his AK-47 with the one hundred round drum. He then switched hands with it and grabbed Fear up by the back of his shirt, pulling him back up to his feet. He looked back and forth over his shoulder, as he walked Fear back to the van. The goon's finger rested on the trigger of his AK-47. He had that mothafucka slightly raised, just in case Italia sprung from behind the ruined car trying to get active.

The goon got Fear into the van with the help of another masked goon. He turned his back to the streets as he was about to hop into the van when he felt a few slugs slam into his back.

He looked over his shoulder and saw Italia blasting at him, a gun in each hand.

Blowl, blowl, blowl, blowl!

The goon jutted forward under the impact of the slugs. Seeing his comrade in trouble, the goon that had pulled Fear into the van turned the full fury of his AK-47 on Italia. Again, she dove behind the car she'd positioned herself behind, allowing it to take the hot lead meant for her. The rapid fire from the AK-47 punctured several holes into the parked vehicle she'd hidden besides, bursting its tires. Lying down beside the car that she'd used as a shield, Italia saw the ankles of the goon she'd shot in the back. She

pointed one of her cannons at his exposed ankles and blew it out from under him.

"Aaaahhh, fuck!" The goon threw his head back hollering in excruciation and crumbling in the street. His comrade that had pulled Fear into the van went to help him, but he fired at him through one of the blown-out windows, keeping him at bay.

"You fucking cunt!" the goon Italia had just dumped at scowled in her direction. He then lifted his AK-47 with the hundred round drum, pointing it and spitting hot fire. The powerful weapon turned the vehicle that Italia was hiding beside into a useless hunk of metal, with all the holes he put in it. "Gaaaaah!" The goon suddenly hollered aloud, feeling fire rip through his ankle. He almost fell until he grabbed hold of the door of the van, preventing himself from hitting the asphalt. Turning around, he shouted to the driver of the van to pull off as he dove inside. The van sped off from the gun battle with the wounded goon hanging halfway out of the sliding door.

"Nuh unh, mothafuckaz!" Italia said with a scowl, having just finished loading up her guns. She sprung to her feet and took off running after the van, both guns up, blazing shots at it. Some of her bullets ricocheted off the back of the van, while others shattered its back windows and blew out its brake lights.

Blowl, blowl, blowl, blowl, blowl, blowl!

Italia ran as fast as she could after the van, ranging shots at it. She wound up blowing out one of the back tires of the van and it swerved out of control, slamming into a light pole. Tucking one of her guns into the front of her jeans, she crept upon the van, making her way over to the driver's window. As she neared the window, she heard the engine trying to turn over as the driver twisted the key in the ignition over and over again.

"Man, start the motherfucker up so we can get the hell from outta here before that crazy bitch shows up again!" The goon that had pulled Fear into the van called out to the driver.

"I'm trying here gotdammit, but this motherfucker won't start." the driver continued to turn the key unsuccessfully.

Italia peeked her head inside of the driver's window and found the man still trying to fire the van up. She took a step back from the van and pointed her gun at the driver, pulling the trigger. The back of the driver's skull exploded, splattering his blood and brain fragments over the windshield and dashboard. Dead, the driver slumped over into the front passenger seat.

With the driver's death came what seemed like a hundred rounds through the side of the van that Italia was on. Once again, she dove to the ground to avoid the life-threatening slugs. Lying on her stomach, she spotted a side view mirror that had been blown off by the wave of bullets. Its reflector was cracked but she could still see herself in it, so she grabbed it.

"Fucking bitch! You're gonna die, you're gonna fucking die, whore!" The goon that had opened fire from inside of the van threatened. Italia could hear him reloading another hundred round drum onto his AK-47 as she crawled around the vehicle. Once she made it to the open door of the van, she placed her back against it, listening to him talk big shit.

"After I kill you, I'm gonna fuck your corpse right in front of your little boyfriend. How would you like that, huh? How would you like that?" The goon cocked his AK-47, pointing it at the back of the van and blowing holes through it. While he was occupied with doing this, Italia eased the side view mirror into the open door of the van, through it she saw the goon shooting up the back of the van. Keeping the side view mirror where it was, she stuck her gun over her shoulder, aiming it precisely. As soon as she pulled the trigger, the goon's head snapped to the right and his brain fragments splattered against the inside of the van. The goon fell to the floor of the vehicle with blood pouring out of his head.

Right then, Italia dropped the side view mirror and climbed into the van. She tucked the gun inside of her jeans beside her other gun and helped Fear out of the van. Pulling an army knife out of her back pocket, she opened it and sliced the zip-cuffs off him. As soon as she did, Fear hugged her lovingly and kissed the top of her head. He then held her face, looking her in her eyes.

"You saved me, ma. You really saved me." He told her.

"I told you I'm your down ass bitch." she capped with a smile.

Fear grinned and then kissed her romantically. At that moment, a helicopter grasped their attention as it lowered to the ground quite fast, causing Italia's hair to ruffle in the air. The power behind the helicopter's spinning propeller also ruffled the couple's clothing. They looked up at the helicopter through narrowed eyelids, meeting another man wearing a ski-mask over his face. The mean looking son of a bitch pointed his pistol grip AK-47, with the drum at them, threateningly.

"Any one of you move and I'll splash your ass." The goon jumped down into the street from the helicopter, AK-47 trained on Fear and Italia, who had their hands up in the air. Behind him, another masked goon appeared toting an AK-47 identical to his. He relieved Italia of the guns on her waistline and stuck them on his waistline. Afterwards, he pulled out a pair of zip-cuffs which he bound Fear and Italia's wrists with, behind their backs. Next, he slipped black pillowcases over their heads and ushered them into the helicopter. Shortly thereafter, the helicopter lifted high into the air and flew across the sky.

The helicopter landed on the rooftop of a building and scattered all of the debris surrounding it. The masked-up goons jumped down out of the bird, grabbing Italia and Fear. Taking their captives by their arm, the goons lead them towards the door of the rooftop. One of the goons pulled out a set of copper and silver keys, using the silver one to open the door. Once the door was opened, the goons ushered the couple inside and down the staircase. Once they reached the landing, Italia and Fear lead down a long corridor, their reflections shown on the waxed floor. The goons stopped at an elevator. One of them pressed the down button on it. Instantly, the elevator dinged, and its double doors slid apart. Everyone walked inside of the elevator, the goon that had opened the rooftop's door, stuck a key with a round end into a slot the same shape below the numbers panel. He turned the key, and something made a click sound. Afterwards, he flipped the square plastic casing covering another button labeled *B* for basement. He punched that button, and then removed his key from out of the slot. The elevator moved downward as he shut the plastic casing shut and stashed the keys inside of his pocket.

Ding!

The elevator sounded once it landed on the basement floor and its double doors opened. The goons lead Fear and Italia down a long ass hallway until they met a large metal door. One of the goons rapped on it and a moment later they heard the door coming unlocked and a large latch being drawn back. The metal door was opened by another goon and Fear and Italia were ushered inside of an enormous room. It had a giant crystal chandelier that hung from the ceiling, an oriental rug that nearly covered up the entire carpeted floor, two chairs sitting at the center and a "60-inch 4K flat screen mounted high up on the wall. There was also a goon posted up in every corner with an AK-47, with mad dog expressions written across their faces.

As soon as the goon planted Fear and Italia in the two chairs sitting at the center of the floor, the double back doors of the dining room opened. Gustavo strolled out, a wicked smile stretched across his face, a framed portrait under his arm.

"Welcome. I'm so glad to see you could make it." Gustavo walked over to Fear and Italia and snatched the black pillowcases off their heads, tossing them aside. He then took the framed portrait from under his arm and shoved it in Fear's face. It was a photo of Master Hahn and Gustavo when they were much younger. They were surrounded by other gangstas in suits and ties. They appeared to be at a banquet or something. "You see this man in this photo? You know him, don't chu?" he tapped his finger against Hahn in the photo. Fear looked up at Gustavo staring him down and then glancing at the portrait. He didn't answer Gustavo. He just gave him the meanest, nastiest look. "Yeah, you know 'em. I believe he trained you. I also believe you didn't tell me that you knew him because you didn't know how I would react which is the only reason why I don't kill you right now. I've been looking for this man for quite some time. You know why? I'll tell you why—" Gustavo told him the story behind his search for Master Hahn. After he finished telling him the story, he beat him on the head with the framed portrait until the glass of it cracked and then broke. The broken glass rained down upon Fear like small diamonds. Gustavo tossed the broken frame aside and Fear shook the glass off him like a wet dog would shake water off his body. "I finally found him, and I had his bitch ass killed!" When he said this, Fear's nostrils flared and he gritted his teeth, veins jumping on his neck and forehead. He breathes heavily with glassy, sorrowful eyes. "What're you gonna do, cry now?"

Fear didn't utter a word, he continued to stare down Gustavo, nostrils flaring, teeth gritting, tears threatening to fall from the brims of his eyes.

"Now, allow me to show you your punishment for not carrying out the order I gave you." Gustavo turned around, pulling a remote control from out of his suit jacket. He turned on the "60-inch 4K flat screen television set mounted on the wall, and dropped his hand beside him, moving out of the way so that Fear and Italia could see what was playing on the T.V.'s monitor.

Fear couldn't believe his eyes as he looked at the television screen. He saw his mother, Verna, standing in the window of an apartment building naked with her mouth duct taped and her wrists bound behind her back. A masked man was standing behind her.

"Oh, no! Oh, God, momma!" Fear called out to his mother as if she could hear him, tears forming in his eyes. His head snapped over to Gustavo who was putting an ear bud inside of his ear so that he could communicate with the masked man,

Lethal, who was also wearing an ear bud underneath his ski mask. "Let her go, you let her go, you mothafucka!" Fear raged with veins bulging on his forehead and spittle flying from off his lips. He was turning red around his ears and face.

"Not just yet, my friend," Gustavo said, coming to stand between Fear and Italia. Italia had tears in her eyes too. She was afraid of what was about to happen to Verna. She loved Fear's mother like she'd pushed her out of her womb, so if anything was to happen to her, she'd feel the full effects of it. There weren't any doubts about that. That was for damn sure.

"Gustavo, I want chu to listen to me, and I want chu to listen to me good, man! If you don't leave my mother be you're gonna—"

Gustavo smacked the dog shit out of Fear and silenced him. "Enough, I won't take threats from the likes of you. Now if you would have done exactly what the fuck, I paid you for, negrito, then this wouldn't be happening now." He looked over to one of his goons. "Duct tape his mouth, and the girls." With the command having been given, a goon duct taped Fear and Italia's mouths, promptly.

Fear shut his eyelids and looked away, but Gustavo grabbed him by the head and forced his eyelids open with his fingers. Fear tried to squeeze his eyelids back shut, but the kingpin's fingers proved to be far stronger than his eyelids.

"No, look, I want chu to see it all. Live with the consequences of your actions. It's not my man that is about to kill your mother, but you, her own fucking son."

Lethal held the back of Verna's neck with one hand and used his other hand to loop a noose around her neck. Having gotten the noose around her neck, the masked man unsheathed a machete from his side. A gleam swept up the full length of the sharp blade and it twinkled at its tip. When Verna seen the machete, she tried to scream but the duct tape over her mouth dead the sound that tried to escape. She thrashed and kicked around seeing Lethal bring the machete near her breasts, terrified of what was going to happen next.

"Hold still, bitch!" Lethal spat as he wrapped his arm around her throat, putting her in a reverse chokehold. He held her tightly against him and sawed away at her saggy breasts, causing a river of blood to spill down her left side. Her right breast dropped and hurled toward the street below, where civilians had gathered to watch the entire thing. Some of them even brought out their camera phones to film the occurrence. Once Verna's right breast had been severed, Lethal sawed away at her left breast. Verna threw her head back screaming at the top of her lung, tears upon tears spilling from the corners of her sorrowful eyes. She tried her best to get away from the madman holding her at knife point, but her efforts were useless. He had her in his clutches and he wasn't about to let go until she was dead.

"Mmmmmmmmm," Verna cried and screamed with the duct tape over her mouth. She threw her body from left to right but she couldn't manage to get loose.

Lethal sheathed the bloody machete on his side and then looked directly into the camera, which was being aimed at him from a helicopter. Lethal grabbed the back of Verna's neck and turned her head so that she'd be facing the camera, waving goodbye at it. The spotlight from the helicopter was shining on them the entire time they were inside of the apartment's window. Right after, Lethal kicked Verna in her ass and she went plummeting downward, camera phones snapping at her from below ground. The wind blew upwards ruffling Verna's hair as she screamed to high heaven, eyes stretched wide open, legs kicking wildly.

"Mmmmmmm!" Fear screamed *no* from behind the duct tape overvhis mouth, horror etched across his face. For the first time in his life, he regretted the choices he'd made, because they all had led him to this moment, which could very well be his mother's death. The tears that pooled in his eyes, dripped from the brims of them.

"Yuuuckkkk!" An ugly noise escaped Verna's lips as she was caught by the snag of the rope. Her face balled up and turned from red to purple, her eyeballs looking like they were about to burst out of their sockets.

Blood clots formed in the whites of her eyes, and veins bulged in her neck and temples. Verna swung from left to right, trying desperately to pull her hands free from the restraints that bound her wrists. "Gagggaggghh!" She gagged horrifically, legs thrashing around wildly as she danced at the end of the rope.

Her eyes bled with her pain and fright, slicking her cheeks wet. Her vision blurred and her head began to feel light. She could feel the hands of death grasp her ankles and pull her toward the other side.

Verna didn't know anything about the life that her son had led, but that meant nothing to the mothafucka that wanted to teach him a lesson. She had always believed that what your child grew to be was a direct reflection of what he was taught. So, hanging from that rope she couldn't help wondering where her and her husband, Big Al, went wrong with raising Fear. She honestly didn't know, but she knew if her life was going to end like this then she would fail him miserably. And that it wasn't him that owed her an apology, but her that owed him one.

FEAR MY GANGSTA 3

She didn't know what he could have done to make a man want to lynch her like he was a Klansman, but she hoped that somehow, in her death, her son found peace, and moved forward to do whatever he had to do to led a fruitful and fulfilling life.

Piss trickled from between Verna's legs as she continued to thrash her legs wildly. After a while her legs started moving slower and slower, and piss dripped from between her legs less and less, until it stopped. Verna twitched every so often before going completely still. She was finally dead.

Lethal peered downward at Verna to see if she'd stopped moving. Having confirmed her death, he motioned for the helicopter to fly over to him. Once it did, he climbed inside of the helicopter and it flew him away, hurriedly, police car sirens bellowing from below.

After witnessing the death of his mother, Fear and Italia bowed their heads. Their entire bodies shook as they cried and whimpered. Heartbroken at what they'd just seen play out before them. A fake sympathetic Gustavo patted Fear on his shoulder and picked up the remote control. He turned the television set off and tossed the remote control aside. He then leaned down into Fear's ear, saying, "The next time you disobey a direct order, especially one I am paying you handsomely for, it'll be you hanging out of the window of some fucking project building. You got that?" Fear didn't answer so Gustavo pulled his head back up by his neck. Gustavo found him crying and looking at him with madness dancing in his pupils. "Yeah, you definitely heard me."

Gustavo walked around to the front of Fear and Italia, shadow looming over them. He took in their sorrowful expressions and felt pleased at the havoc he'd wreaked on their lives. Standing there before them, he reached inside of his suit and pulled out a pair of latex gloves. He placed his hands inside of the gloves one at a time, flexing his fingers inside of them as he pulled them down over his wrists.

Gustavo looked at the double doors at the back of the room and whistled. Right then, one of Gustavo's goons rolled out a little boy who was strapped to a dolly. The little guy looked like Hannibal Lecter, except he had a gag over his mouth, not a muzzle. The goon rolled the boy over to Gustavo, stopping him before Fear and Italia, leaving him facing the young couple. "Do you remember this cute lil' fella, Alvin?" Gustavo ruffled the top of the boy's head causing him to whimper. The little boy tried to scream over and over again, but the gag stopped the sound from escaping.

Fear looked the boy in his face. It dawned on him. The little guy was Esteban's kid.

"Yessss, you remember him, don't chu? It's time I complete the task that cho bitch ass couldn't finish." Gustavo said as he took a small bottle that looked like insulin would come inside of and a syringe. He stuck the needle through the top of the small bottle and pulled the plunger, withdrawing the contents of the bottle. The shaft of the syringe quickly filled up with what looked like a bright, lime green substance. Gustavo pulled the boy's neck aside as he cried; he then injected him with half of the needle's contents. The boy lay back on the dolly with vacant eyes and a wide-open mouth. Fear looked at the kid; he was dead.

"Now, it's the fiancée's turn." Gustavo moved towards Italia with the needle containing the deadly substance. Her eyelids peeled wide open, and she struggled to get free from her restraints, whipping her head from left to right.

"Nooooooo!" Fear screamed as loud as he could with the duct tape over his mouth, vein threatening to erupt from his temple.

To Be Continued...

Fear My Gangsta 4

Kill or be Killed

AVAILABLE NOW BY TRANAY ADAMS

The Devil Wears Timbs 1-7

Bury Me A G 1-5

Fear My Gangsta 1-5

The Last of The Ogs 1-3

King of Trenches 1-3

The Realest Killaz 1-3

These Scandalous Streets 1-3

A Hood Nigga's Blues

A Gangsta's Empire 1-4

A South-Central Love Affair

Me And My Hittas 1- 6

The Last Real Nigga Alive 1-3

A Hood Nigga's Blues

Bloody Knuckles

Fangeance

COMING SOON BY TRANAY ADAMS

Bloody Knuckles 2

They Made Me An Animal

Dope Land

www.ingramcontent.com/pod-product-compliance
Lightning Source LLC
LaVergne TN
LVHW051951060526
838201LV00059B/3600